THE *I AM*

PRAISE FOR *I AM MARGARET*

BR⚡THERS

CORINNA TURNER

unSeen

First published by Unseen Books in 2017
An Imprint of Zephyr Publishing*

ISBN: 978-1-910806-60-9 (paperback)

Also available as an eBook

* Zephyr Publishing, UK—Corinna Turner, T/A

**_Thanks must also go to the generous developers of these
beautiful Open Source fonts:_**
_Quattrocentro Roman, Source Sans Pro, Note This, DESTROY,
WC Rhesus A Bta, Almendra, and Rosario._

If we have died with him, then we shall live with him.

2 Tim 2:11

JOE

I'd spent thirteen years very happily—but so ignorantly—alive and at no point had I studied the art of illegal border crossing. I'd totally taken life for granted. *Everything*, in fact. But *K* had spent quite a few of his eighteen years preparing for this journey. And he'd taken good care of me so far...

So when he drew me away from the narrow slit where the tarpaulin side was unfastened from the end of the lorry trailer against which we were sitting, I didn't resist, though I'd been watching the end of the Channel Bridge coming closer, peeping at the guard towers up ahead, the big barriers—open at the moment, thankfully—and the soldiers, on guard beside them...

But in the dim glow from the bridge lights I saw K place a finger to his lips, then point to our eyes and make a rapid gesture towards and then away from them... oh, he meant that torches could reflect off them and give us away. No looking out, then.

That was *hard*, though. In fact, it was almost unbearable. Like some form of torture... My hands clenched together, tighter and tighter, as I pictured the French end of the bridge coming nearer and nearer...

"They don't usually stop many vehicles," K murmured, not for the first time. "We'll be okay."

But as my shoulder pressed against his arm in the darkness, I could feel the faint, rhythmic muscle movements that said his fingers were keeping tally as he prayed. Huh. From a factual point of view it was fascinating learning all the things the EuroGov were so scared of everyone knowing, but I wasn't usually very interested in the *praying* side of K's God-stuff, considering how I felt about fathers and mothers right now—but just at this moment I found myself *hoping* very hard indeed.

Don't let them stop us. Don't let them stop us...

The Channel Bridge was the only really dangerous chokepoint between here and Vatican State. Well, entering Rome itself was going to be dodgy, but K had procedures to contact people who could deal with all that. We just had to get there.

And if we made it across this bridge, surely we would...

I could tell Joe was scared. Well, he might only be thirteen, but he was no fool. I tried my hardest to *feel* calm and unconcerned, because feelings were contagious, after all. What I'd just said was true—unless there was an alert in place, they *didn't* stop much traffic for inspection. They did so like to make a big thing about how the EuroBloc was just one large country, after all.

Our lorry had slowed right up to pass through the barrier area. A searchlight played on the side, moving from front to back in a downright sinister manner.

My heart pounded harder and harder. If they stopped us... If they stopped us, it would mean Joe's life. Mine too, but for me the stakes were higher still. My life, *and* my *sister's* life, *and* my *parent's* lives, *and* Lord only knew how many others...

Lord, please don't let them stop us... Please don't let them stop us...

I realized how tense I'd become and started trying to relax again. *They hardly stop any vehicles. They hardly stop any vehicles...*

Soldier's voices... we must've reached the barrier...

The lorry carried on moving, but it was only crawling now. Joe pressed closer to me, so I slipped an arm around him, trying to breathe slowly and calmly...

Crawling... crawling... still moving... and...

The lorry began to accelerate. We'd made it through the checkpoint. *Thank you, Lord! Thank you...* I couldn't help letting my head fall back with a slight sigh of relief. I gave Joe's shoulders a squeeze and caught his blazing smile just before we left the bridge lights behind us and were plunged into darkness.

"Right," I murmured. "Time for some supper."

Joe tensed again—in eagerness, this time. Like most boys his age, he was always hungry. So was I, just at the moment. But I couldn't help suspecting that the simple provision of regular meals had been quite instrumental in earning Joe's guarded trust!

I crossed myself and said grace, smiling in the darkness as Joe mumbled an automatic 'Amen'. How baffled he'd been the first time I'd done this!

"What are you doing?" he'd asked.

"Saying thank you for the food."

"But who are you *thanking?*" he'd demanded.

That had been our first conversation about God, come to think of it.

"But everyone knows God doesn't *exist,*" he'd announced with all the certainty a thirteen-year-old could muster, which was rather a lot.

"Oh? How do they know that?"

He'd opened his mouth... and stopped. "Well... the teacher said," he offered at last. With rather less certainty. "It was in the textbook, too," he added, even more doubtfully.

"Did the teacher—and the charming EuroGov textbook—also say that children like you needed to be dismantled for the greater good of society?"

Silence.

Utter silence.

Still smiling slightly at the memory, I opened my backpack and fished around for food. We'd been able to buy it freely from small towns with market stalls that didn't require ID cards for purchases, and I'd made sure we had plenty before we stowed away in the lorry.

The secret to a successful trip like this, so 'Cousin' Mark had told me often enough, was to make a clean getaway—i.e. no pursuit—and have plenty of money. The unexpected presence of a preSort-age child had complicated things, but thankfully the funds were holding out okay. The clean getaway... certainly *seemed* to have been achieved, though in the circumstances that seemed near-miraculous. Did it just.

Goodness knew I *hoped* it had really been achieved... If not... I swallowed painfully. If not, Margo and my parents might already be arrested... might already be *dead.* Their safety relied entirely on me not getting caught. No, not even merely *not being caught.* Not being *identified* in any way...

"We *have* got enough food?" Joe sounded anxious, alarmed by my inactivity.

"Plenty, plenty." I dragged my attention from the fears and worries that had dogged me like a toxic cloud ever since I left Salperton—imagined stuffing them into the Lord's hands and leaving them there—and passed Joe a couple of slices of bread and some cheese. "Don't you remember that story about the loaves and fishes?"

"That was cool," said Joe. I guess just at the moment, magic multiplying food was something that stuck in his memory rather well. "Probably just a story, though."

"What if it wasn't?" I'd never really been able to speak to anyone about my faith, for obvious reasons. Joe was proving something of a crash-course in evangelization for me. Not that he was exactly evangelized, though the Lord surely knew I was trying my best. Was this some sort of providential preparation for my vocation?

Joe shrugged. "Be even cooler then. Can't you multiply this bread and cheese for me?" The question was half challenging—but half... hopeful? Just a shade.

"Sorry," I said, biting into my own somewhat meager meal. "That's rather a rare ability. But I don't think that event is supposed to make us think we can just click our fingers ourselves and magic up food—even though some saints have done pretty much that, just occasionally. It's supposed to show us that if we trust in Him, He will always provide us with what we need."

I just glimpsed Joe frowning in the low light. "Like... you turning up when I needed you?"

I beamed, unseen by Joe, who was focused on the food. "Yes, exactly." Except...

"Couldn't He have just got my parents to follow the rules in the first place, then?"

The tight thread of pain in that seemed to whip around my guts and constrict them viciously. Clear enough what he was thinking: *then I'd be at home right now, and none of this would have happened.*

"Well, that's the thing about what I just said. He gives us what we *need*. Not what we *think* we need. Not what we *want. Sometimes* all three are the same. But sometimes they aren't. And we may not understand why something was actually what we needed until we're face to face with Him. Sometimes one is just left scratching one's head and wondering why, *how* is this what I need, how?"

Joe frowned even harder. "Then how do you know He's even there at all? I mean, maybe it's just random chance?"

"Because sometimes you can see the reasons, the chains of events, especially with hindsight. Holier people are better at it. Anyway, random chance doesn't account for things like multiplying loaves."

"I wish you *could* do that." Half Joe's food was gone already.

I smiled. "Sorry. I can only..." I hesitated. What I was about to say was kind of private. I mean, my family had figured it out, but I'd always been shy talking about it to other people. "Well, I do get a flicker of prophecy. Just now and then. Sort of a... feeling. When talking to God. Not all the time. Evidence against your 'random chance' idea, but we can't eat it, I'm afraid."

Joe looked up from his food at last, peering intently at my face in the darkness. Oh, trying to tell if I was having him on. Great, I bared my soul to him and he just wondered if I was pranking him. I smothered a sigh.

"So... *are* we going to get to Rome?" he demanded eventually. Giving me the benefit of the doubt? "Did it tell you to get on *this* lorry? Is that how you picked it?" His voice grew eager as he spoke.

I did sigh, though, at that. "I told you, it's only now and then. I picked this lorry with a God-given gift, it's true, but it was my intellect. When I pray about our trip—manage to *properly* pray, that is, you know, settle myself, not just thinking, *help, help us, Lord,* well, I just feel... peace. And love. Like God really loves us both. Nothing else, really."

It was Joe's turn to give a huge sigh. "We can't just *not eat it,*" he exclaimed rather melodramatically, "it doesn't seem to be any use *at all!*"

I shrugged. "We aren't puppets, remember? God doesn't promise never to let bad things happen to us, he just promises to bring good things out of them. God's priorities are totally different from ours, anyway. Think what an ant's priorities must be like, compared to ours? Pretty small and narrow and stupid, right? Well, with God, *we're* the ants."

"Huh." I wasn't sure Joe liked being an ant, much, but he fell silent, munching on his second slice of bread and cheese, so I tucked in properly as well.

A few glimpses through the slit as we drove showed large highways, quiet at this time of night, and lots of big lorry parks. Back at Dover I'd made very sure we got into a trailer already attached to a lorry from the Swiss department, though. If things went well, maybe we would get all the way over the first part of the Alps before we had to part company with it.

I'd specifically avoided an Italian lorry. They got stopped and searched about six times more often than any other nationality, according to Father Mark...

But Swiss lorries, no more than any other kind.

JOE
We got over the bridge! Soon enough that thought was running through my mind as I scoffed the last of my bread and cheese, despite the strange conversation about prophecy and K not being able to multiply food. *We got across.* There was nothing between us and the Vatican, and a ship to the African Free States! And... the rest of my life!

Well... okay, over a thousand kilometers of EuroBloc stretched out between us and the rest of my life, but all the same. Surely that was the worst bit over? Hopefully we could just sit here, nap, and eat, and in, what—forty-eight hours or so?—we'd be in the Swiss Department.

If we could manage to stow away again, we might even make it to Rome by the next day, but we'd probably have to walk. That was how we'd gotten from Yorkshire down to Dover, using footpaths and off-road trails. In all, it took us almost three weeks, but we'd had no serious alarms and even if he still wouldn't tell me his full name, I'd come to trust K more than I really felt was wise. I mean, after what my parents did, what hope was there that *anyone* could be trusted?

All the same, K was smart. He'd delayed his own flight until after the summer holidays— apparently the time when most SortEvaders fled, hoping to blend in with summer backpackers, who were for this reason regularly stopped and ID'ed. Posing as a New Adult on a weekend hike, he'd aimed to stay well off-road in the week—doubly important once he found himself stuck with school-age me.

Each day of the weekend—Friday evening through to Sunday—he'd hidden me in the forest near a town and gone in on his own, buying only a modest amount of food each time, but after he'd done it several times we'd always had enough for the week ahead. Just about. No prizes for guessing who'd carried most of it. I wasn't exactly big for my age. Each time, I'd been watching the road like a hawk from my hiding place, terrified he'd give me the slip...

But on one occasion I'd strayed too far into the woods near our camp and got lost, and rather than thanking his God and slipping away he'd actually searched until he found me. So maybe K really wouldn't desert me too readily. Even though nothing but chance, and a really inconvenient chance it had been for him, had landed him with me. Perhaps it was because I didn't have a brother that I'd been tricked into partial trust, despite...

A *father* figure, now, no chance...

I shook the memory away. *Again.*

My meal was gone. I almost asked for more but stopped myself. K had only planned and saved enough for one on this trip. The money wasn't endless, and he didn't have the knack of multiplying food! I couldn't help shaking my head, amused by my sensible self-restraint. Three weeks ago such behavior wouldn't even have occurred to me. I'd probably have whined for more, in fact, if my mum had said no...

My mum... Who *lied.* My whole life...

A massive yawn cracked my jaws and again I pushed away the thoughts of my former life in favor of scooting down, knees drawn up in the tiny space, propping my feet up on my rucksack, much smaller and lighter than K's, and resting my head on his legs, which didn't really make a better pillow than the rucksack, but prevented him from sneaking off without me. 'Cause my brain knew the trust was stupid, even if my heart didn't.

"K?" Something I'd been meaning to ask him for *ages* popped back into my head.

"Umhum?"

"Are there railways in Africa?" They'd never really covered Africa much in school. Or on telly. The EuroGov didn't like the African Free States very much. Too many Believers. K would fit right in.

Except *he* didn't want to go on to Africa, did he? He wanted to stay in the Vatican State and train to be an honest-to-goodness underground *priest*. Suicidal, or what? Perhaps he'd change his mind and come with me. I really hoped so. For his sake... and yeah, mine too. Except... I couldn't forget how he'd described it to me. Described *why* he was doing it...

"Yes. Some of the longest railway lines in the world, I think," K replied.

I smiled in the darkness. Good. I was glad to know that.

"And I'm sure they need train drivers," added K slyly.

I could hear that he was smiling too, but I didn't mind. I mean, we were off to *Africa—both of us, please, please, please?*—where I would one day drive cutting edge electric locomotives—or possibly quainter, older ones—across vast expanses—Africa was *big*, right?—crossing massive sunsets that took up half the sky, maybe having to stop for elephants, and look out for lions...

By the time K had dug my foil blanket out of his rucksack and started tucking it over me, I was almost asleep. The familiar *rustle-rustle* lulled me right off, that and the clackety-clack of train wheels in my head...

K

I fought to stay awake, since both of us sleeping whilst in this lorry-trap seemed a bad idea of monumental proportions, but it was hard. Sitting in the darkness, the lorry swaying gently, exhaustion pressing on me... Eventually I resorted to pinching the backs of my hands, harder and harder. I had to stay awake. Our lives depended on it. My *family's* lives depended on it...

I pictured my fifteen-year-old sister, Margaret—Margo, as we all called her. So bright, yet she was a Borderline, just because she was bad at Math. Dyscalculia, her condition was called: Math dyslexia. If she failed her Sorting tests, she'd be sent to the Facility to be dismantled for spare parts to cure those perfect enough to be granted adult status—which was what they wanted to do to Joe. But only just a Borderline, surely? She always said no one at school even realized. And she had three more years—well, two and a half—to get her Math up to the required level, before her Sorting tests at eighteen. And a really good teacher. Uncle Peter could teach Math to *dogs and cats*.

"Why didn't you bring her with you?" Joe had asked me, when I first revealed my sister M's Borderline status.

"She's confident she'll pass," I'd told him. "She wouldn't leave without B, anyway. He's her best friend. She wants to marry him someday."

Joe had rolled his eyes at this romantic notion, making me grin. But then he'd said, "Wouldn't he come with her? If *he* wants to marry *her*."

That'd pulled me up short for a moment or two. Because Bane, oh, hot-headed Bane, with a relationship with his own family several degrees below zero, he would have been prepared to run away in a heartbeat. Especially if it helped Margo...

"She has a chance at a normal life," I'd tried to explain. "Why would she want to throw that away?"

"Did you ask her to come?"

"Not flat out," I admitted. "I never got the impression she *wanted* to."

"Or that's what she wanted you to think. We both know how dangerous it is for you having a preSort-age kid along—I expect she knew that too."

Joe's quiet words had haunted me every mile of the way since then. Had Margo simply pretended that the idea of fleeing the EuroBloc didn't interest her simply to avoid burdening me with her incriminating teen self? That would be just like her...

And the worst thing was, there was absolutely *nothing* I could do about it now. Except not get caught, and trust in the Lord.

And in Bane...

Sleep was tugging at me again. Along with a sensation

I'd become very familiar with since meeting Joe—pins and needles. In my leg. As usual. I tried wiggling my toes, slowly and gently, but even that much made Joe stir, his fingers knotting even tighter into my trouser fabric. I desisted, and he settled, dropping back into deeper sleep.

Poor kid. My heart bled for him. Actually, on a purely selfish level, despite the added dangers and difficulties created by his presence, I loved having him along. It was like having a little brother. I'd always wanted a little brother—I mean, not instead of Margo, I wouldn't have *swapped* her for the world, but *as well as* would've been good. No hope of that, with the EuroBloc Genetics' Department's strict breeding laws. Except now, and thanks to *them*—ha ha, so there, EGD!—I did.

Perhaps if Joe could come to consider me *his* brother, it would help heal the deep wounds inflicted on him that fatal evening three weeks ago when his world was so completely shattered. Though to heal, above all, he needed to forgive... *Lord, I'm trying to help him to understand that. Please give me the right words...*

He drank in faith *facts* like a sponge, clearly fascinated, but any mention of God's love or God as Father was met with steely resistance. Go figure.

How keen he was to get to Africa, to freedom and wide open skies and, well, *trains*, but... I couldn't help hoping that maybe, somehow, he could stay in Vatican State. I'd a nasty feeling I'd heard that all unaccompanied children were sent on to Africa as a matter of course, but... there were several cadet corps. Swiss Guard cadets was out, of course, since Joe was as British as I was, but the Vatican Police Cadets or something? I was pretty sure I'd also heard that the absolute youngest you could be to be admitted to the cadets was fifteen, so that was still a problem...

I suppose if Joe accepted me as his big brother by the time we got there, he wouldn't exactly *be* an unaccompanied child, would he? Well, I'd still stow us away on another lorry if the opportunity presented, since the sooner we got there the safer for both of us, but I couldn't help almost hoping that we'd have to walk again... Give Joe that little bit more time to come to trust me, despite his understandable paranoia...

But then... if I did have a vocation, four years and I'd be ordained and on my way, and then what about Joe? But to Joe, four years were almost a third of his life. Four more years, and he'd be almost my age. Grown-up. Worrying about probably having to leave him in four years was stupid. He'd be old enough for Africa and *trains* by then, anyway. Right *now*, he just needed steadfast, reliable TLC, that's what he needed. And unless I was totally barking up the wrong tree with this vocation of mine, if he was going to get it from me, he needed to stay in the Vatican. And I kind of hoped he was going to get it from me.

My belated little brother, such an utterly unexpected gift from God...

Such a heavy responsibility too, though I did not begrudge him that.

My eyes felt so heavy, despite the increasing discomfort in my leg. I really didn't want to disturb Joe, though. The constant walking was tougher for him than for me, and he tried so hard not to slow me down...

No! I jerked back from a doze at the last minute. No, I must not sleep. Not tonight. I should concentrate on my leg, maybe that would wake me up.

Okay, concentrating on the leg was not such a good idea. The pins and needles were getting really vicious.

Offer it up, huh? For Joe's healing and for a safe journey. What are you complaining about, anyway? This is nothing. Think of it as practice for the all-too-likely reward for your priestly work.

Conscious Dismantlement...

Normally I pushed thoughts of *that* away at once, but I desperately needed to wake up, so for once I allowed my mind to follow the thread...

Could anything really count as *practice* for Conscious Dismantlement? Just at the thought of it, my heart was pounding harder, sweat squeezing out onto my suddenly cold forehead. I felt icy right through, in fact. Yes, I tried not to think about it too much—because whenever I did, things suddenly looked *very* different.

I mean, what was I *doing?* I was a New Adult, I'd passed

my Sorting, I'd gotten great exam results just two months back, I'd had everything before me... A scholarship to university, excellent job prospects... maybe I could one day have even found myself earning enough to afford a third child...

And I'd thrown it all away. Thrown it away by faking my death and risking my life on this perilous journey to the Vatican, all so that I could spend four hyper-hyper-intense years of study, and *that* all so I could return to the EuroBloc for an all too brief ministry ending in... in a slow, agonizing, tortuous death as every organ was harvested from my conscious, still-breathing body. That or risk damnation by apostasy should my courage fail me...

Lord, why am I doing this? My mind-whisper was confused, chilled, bewildered...

The answer came at once, like a warm breath into my fearful soul: *Because I did the same for you.*

Ah yes, He'd done the same for me. How could I not risk the same, for the sake of His beloved children, *my* own brothers and sisters...?

My breathing steadied a little, and the chill fear eased— leaving me shivering and clammy. What a big brave priest I was going to make...

Lord... Lord... now this was a prayer I had prayed for years... *Lord, if I'm not strong enough, please don't lead me to that choice. I beg You... Let the seminary turn me down, let me study for four years and then be turned down for ordination, let me be ordained but sent to Africa, but let me not be brought to that moment unless I will be strong enough to stand. I beg You...*

For I simply do not know if I can open myself to accept Your strength in that most dire moment of need, or whether, in the dread and terror of it all, I will simply rely on myself...

And fall...

JOE
"Joe! Wake up!" K was shaking my shoulder, hard. "We're being pulled over!"

"What?" My eyes flew open. It wasn't dark, now. Light blazed around the front of the lorry, and blue and red lights flashed from behind. "But you said..."

"I don't know why it's happening, but it is! We've got to jump and run. We mustn't be caught!"

He didn't need to tell *me* that! With a loud *rustle-rustle* that only we could possibly hear over the engines, he crammed my blanket back into his rucksack and fastened it, heaved it on. He never ever removed his gloves, but he yanked a balaclava down over his face. I did the same. As he'd explained early on, in the circumstances, there was just a slight risk that identifying *me* might put them onto *K.*

K was craning his neck to get the best look outside that he could without actually showing himself, jiggling one leg up and down as his fingers unfastened more of the tarpaulin to enlarge the slit.

"Argh!" he hissed. "I think it's just a random check, but the police car is herding us into a floodlit area they've set up for the night. Police cars around it, one army truck with soldiers. Blasted French Resistance are always busy..." he added under his breath, in explanation, then went on firmly, "We've got to jump as soon as we've slowed enough, before we're surrounded. I can see forest; we run straight into it and keep going, okay? Ready?"

I swallowed. I was shaking, but I knew K was right. Jump and run like heck was our only chance. Oh *why* did they have to choose *our* lorry?

"Now!" K dropped out through the slit and ran alongside, waiting for me. I forced myself to move, slipping through and jumping to the road. My feet came down hard and I stumbled, but K grabbed my shoulder, steadying me.

"Come on!" he whispered, gripping my arm, pulling me after him. I got my feet sorted out and started to run in earnest, at right angles away from the lorry. The police car following let off its siren, beeping the horn madly. They'd seen us...

We ran on.

Shouts in Esperanto from the army truck—"*Halt!*"

Yeah, right! The forest loomed ahead, we'd nearly reached it. I drove my feet into the tarmac, running

13

absolutely as fast as I could, though K's longer stride meant he was half-towing me behind him...

Crack! Crack!

Panic exploded inside me... *Gunshots! They're really shooting at me? Can't they see I'm just a kid? Oh no, run, Joe, run...*

K pushed me along ahead of him, now; somehow he'd gotten behind me... but the forest was only a few strides away... We were going to make...

Something slammed into the small of my back with incredible force, sending me sprawling on the road... my chin skidded painfully along the tarmac... oww... I needed to jump right up again, and run, run, run... My mind planned it, yet somehow when I finally came to a halt, I couldn't seem to move... Just lay in a numb, swimming, echoing dullness.

Get up, Joe! Get up and run! Why am I lying here like this?

K

Something plucked at my sleeve and my trouser leg, spinning me off balance and almost bringing me crashing down on Joe, but I caught myself just in time and threw myself beside him in a more controlled manner.

"*Come on, Joe!*" I was horribly sure that he'd been hit, but there was no time to even *look*. Dragging his arm over my shoulder, I pulled him to his feet. I glimpsed his face in the lights, pale and confused, but his legs moved feebly as he struggled to help me...

Crack... Another bullet yanked at my sleeve, but drag-carrying Joe, I'd taken the last few strides and we were in among the trees. Solid, bullet-proof... Not close enough together, though...

From the sounds of shouting and clanking and thumping, many of the soldiers were still getting themselves together, but the couple who'd been shooting were rushing towards our sanctuary. No time to stop, no time to do *anything*. But Joe was slumped against me, his chest heaving weakly, clearly unable to even stand...

I hefted him up, over the top of my shoulder and

backpack, and began to run.

Oh God, don't let it end like this... Don't let it end like this!

3 Weeks Earlier

Salperton-Under-Fell, Yorkshire, British Department, EuroBloc

JOE

"Can't we watch the program about railway signals?" I asked Dad, as he selected the motor racing. "It starts in five minutes on the technology channel."

"The race will still be on, Joe."

"But it's important! It's really competitive becoming a train driver! I'll have to prove that I've been interested for ages and know loads!"

"You don't have to know loads beforehand," said Dad—like always. "That's what training is for. Anyway, you're..."

"...rather young to be thinking about career paths." I mouthed it with him. It must've been a boy/girl thing, because whenever my little sister Daisy started talking about how she wanted to be a midwife one day, all she'd get was encouragement, and she was almost three years younger than me. All I ever got was encouragement *not* to think ahead.

I sighed, flopped back on the sofa and tried to watch the race. Daisy was already in bed, so there wasn't much else to do. It would be more interesting with signals. And tracks. And *timetables*. All the stupid cars did was drive in circles. As usual. Eventually one of them crashed and a wheel flew off. The driver jumped out and waved to the camera. *Still alive, yay...* Now there was a stupid career, and a half. Driving in circles, trying to get killed. Dad wished he was a racing car driver, though. I could tell from the way he stared at the screen, like he wanted to get inside it.

The camera had gone back to following the cars that still had wheels on when I heard an even more boring normal car pulling up outside our house. I glanced at the clock. Almost eight. Were we expecting a visitor?

The doorbell chimed, followed by the sound of Mum heading out of the kitchen to answer it. I got up and lurked by the lounge doorway to listen. More interesting than cars.

"Hello, are you Karen Whitelow?" The man's voice was calm and professional.

A really long, odd silence greeted this normal enough question. When Mum finally spoke, her voice was tight and strained, like she could hardly get it out. "Who... *who are you?*"

"We're from the EGD, Mrs. Whitelow. UnRegistered Child 6349531 is required to attend Salperton Facility tonight, and we have been sent to provide escort. Is unRegistered Child 6349531 in the house? May I remind you that any attempt to obstruct an EGD official in the course of their duties carries a charge of Sedition: Category 2 and will result in the immediate removal of any other child. Now, where is unRegistered Child 6349531?"

What on earth was this guy going on about? I peeped around into the hall in time to see Mum, her face the most ghastly white I'd ever seen it, raise a trembling finger and point silently towards the lounge. Our eyes met but she jerked hers away, her face crumpling.

A big man in a grey civilian uniform pushed past her, followed by a slightly less brawny guy holding a clipboard. Both had pistols at their belts. *Whoa.* Who were they? What had the guy said? EGD... that and the reference to unRegistered meant... EuroBloc Genetics Department. Bad guys. But they'd obviously come to the wrong house. Why didn't Mum just send them away?

Their eyes fixed on me. "Are you Joe Whitelow?"

Why did they know all our names? My skin prickled, uneasily. "Yes..."

"Good." The man muttered to his clipboard-wielding companion, "Put him in the car."

What? No way... I skipped backwards into the safety of the lounge, where Dad was. "I'm not unRegistered! Dad? Dad, these idiots think I'm unRegistered!"

But Dad was sitting motionless in his chair, his eyes still glued to the television, but now they were totally unfocussed, like he couldn't even see the cars on the screen.

The big man reached for me and I darted behind Dad's chair, shaking his shoulder. "Dad! Tell these idiots they've come to the wrong house! Tell them!"

"If you're Joe Whitelow, unRegistered Child 6349531, then we have not come to the wrong house," said the big man impatiently, advancing towards me.

"Dad!" I yelled, but he just *sat there.* I'd have to tell them myself... "Yes, you *have!* I am not unRegistered! My parents are *Registered!* Since before I was born! Just look it up! My mum can get out the Registration certificate... They're Registered!"

But even as I spoke, I realized that having parents who were Registered when you were *born* wasn't good enough. They had to be Registered when you were *conceived*... For the first time an icy finger of doubt stroked my spine. I couldn't actually be unRegistered, could I? How could they not have *told* me?

"Come on..." The big man reached for me again. I evaded his grab and raced to the back door. Dad just sat there, doing nothing... I had to get away! I turned the key in the lock and yanked the door open, hurtled out... straight into the grasp of a third man in grey. In a trice, he'd grabbed both my wrists, snapped a pair of handcuffs onto them, and was bundling me back through the door.

"Got him, sir," he said.

"Good. Let's go."

They walked me through the kitchen, to the hall. They were going to put me in that car, drive me to the Facility and... Everyone knew unRegistered kids got taken straight to the Lab and dismantled right away. By morning all my organs would be packed in medBags en route to some hospital freezer...

Terror overwhelmed me—gasping, I began to struggle as hard as I could, fighting them every step of the way...

"Oh, stop it," said the big man. "It's not like you're going to feel anything. Not one thing. Only the very worst superstitious idiots get *Conscious* Dismantlement, you must know *that*. And it's a top notch lab, of course, everything hospital grade."

Not going to feel anything? Hospital grade? What did that *matter?* They were going to *kill* me! They were going to...

My stomach convulsed, and I threw up over the man's feet and Mum's clean carpet. My mum... still standing hunched by the door, not looking at me.

The man gave his boots an impatient shake and dragged me onwards, saying nastily, "Waterproof and washable, unRegistered Child. Do your worst."

We were almost to the front door, and all my struggles

were achieving nothing. I was just a short, skinny thirteen-year-old...

"Dad!" I screamed. "Dad, help me! Help me! Mum! Do something! Do something, *please!*"

She did. She began to cry. Great shaking sobs, her head still down. Still not looking at me.

"Mum!" They were dragging me down the steps... "Dad! Dad! HELP ME! HELP ME! DAD! *DAD!*" I was shrieking it at the top of my lungs. He had to help me! He had to! He was *Dad!* Any moment now! Any moment he'd come sprinting out of the house and give it to these men! He'd save me!

"DAD!"

But they were opening the rear door of the car... there were grilles over the back windows... one guy got in... they were pushing me after him... the other guy was getting in beside me... *"DAD! MUM! HELP ME! HELP M..."* The door slammed shut.

Mum still stood in the doorway, still hunched, still shaking. Dad must still be sitting like a statue in the lounge. It was true. I was unRegistered. They'd lied... my whole life...

The car started. Clipboard man was the driver, the other two were in the back, sandwiching me.

"*Joe!*" Finally, I heard someone calling my name—Daisy came rushing out of the door. Mum grabbed for her but missed... Daisy leaped down the steps and ran towards the car, but we were pulling away. She chased after us, yelling all the time: "Joe! *Joe!* Where are they taking you? *Joe! Bring him back... Bring him back!*"

But of course the men just drove right on.

K

I glanced at my rucksack, placed carefully out of the way at the edge of the forest, and drew a deep, steadying breath. This was it. My exact body weight in pork was strapped into the driver's seat of the battered old car. The seam of the hydrogen tank had been weakened, just enough. *Oh Lord, let it be just enough!* Everything was ready. This was the moment I'd been saving for, and planning for, and praying about—on and off—since I was thirteen years old and had finally accepted that the beautiful, deadly call to the priesthood really was stirring in my heart.

If I did this, there was no going back...

If I did this? I shook my head, a slight snort of laughter escaping me. I might stand here and indulge in a few moments of solemn, doubt-ridden angst, but there was no real question that I was going to *do it.*

Now I just had to wait for the Fellest road to be clear, ease the car back onto it and set it going. Two sets of headlights were currently in sight, though, so I'd have to let them go by. The *obvious* thing would have been to wait until the middle of the night, of course, when there was no traffic—which was precisely why I wasn't doing that.

No one would be suspicious of a crash at barely quarter past eight in the evening...

JOE

...My parents hadn't just lied. They'd done *nothing.* Nothing to save me. Some people fled to Africa with their unRegistered child, didn't they? Saved them...

But *they* hadn't saved *me.* They'd just said nothing and waited for the knock at the door. Lied, and so not even given me a chance to try and save *myself...*

I was too young, of course. To have any real chance on my own. I was so obviously preSort-Age. But at least I'd have had a *chance.* Except... I'd have had to take Daisy with me, wouldn't I, or they'd have taken her in my place... And Daisy was even younger and more noticeable than me...

Mum and Dad should have arranged it... Taken us *both.* So much safer with adults along...

But they hadn't. They'd just waited.

What chance did I have now, trapped in the back of this car, being driven straight to the Facility and their precious hospital-grade Lab?

The answer to that question caused panic to rise up and choke me, so that I could hardly think at all as the car sped out of Salperton and into the forest.

Get it together, Joe, I told myself. *Get it together and try to* think.

I had to escape. I simply had to, or I was dead!

I eyed the two EGD men. I didn't know much about the EGD, but from the civilian cut of their uniforms—as opposed to military—I'd a feeling they were EGD inspectors, not Facility Security Guards. Maybe even Facility Guards didn't relish dragging one hundred percent normal, healthy kids to their deaths...

What sort of pistols did they have? Probably nonLethal. The last thing they'd want to do was kill me. Not outside of the Lab.

Could I grab one, and... But they were watching me. And there were two of them. Even if I actually somehow managed to shoot *one* of them, the other would overpower me. And the driver would just drive right on. And I couldn't get to *him* because there was a sliding Perspex window, like in a taxi.

Going for the guns was no use. And I couldn't think of anything else.

Was I... really going to die, tonight?

K

This was it! No headlights in sight. Sitting awkwardly in the lap of pork-me, I drove back onto the main road, scrambled out, and readied the carefully crafted brace for the accelerator. Steering wheel first... the road was dead straight here, going along to a bend with a fantastic outcrop of rock that ought to be more than a match for the hydrogen tank's dodgy seam... *Lord, let it be so!*

I fastened the bungees to the wheel, then, holding the clutch down very carefully with one hand, I wedged the brace into position. The engine rose to a scream...

Get ready... O Lord, grant me success!

I scooted back to arm's length... then snatched my hand clear...

The car was off with a squeal of tires, the driver's door slamming shut under the force of its acceleration... I just remembered to dart back into the forest and take up position behind the nice explosion-proof tree I'd picked, before peeping out...

The car was going straight down the road, not veering much yet... *Thank you, Lord...*

Looking good...

Wait... it was starting to drift slightly... Oh no! Would it reach the crag in time? Because if it didn't explode...

Lord have mercy, if it didn't explode, my whole family and half the people we knew would die...

Lord, please keep it on the road!

JOE

I was shaking, vibrating like a train speeding over cross-tracks. *I'm going to die tonight...* The words kept running through my mind... *I'm going to die, I'm going to die...* clackety-clackety, louder and louder, roaring in my ears like a run-away train... *I'm going to die, I'm going to die...* and I was stuck on the tracks in front of it, helpless, couldn't get away... *I'm going to die, I'm going to die, I'mgoingtodie, I'mgoingtodie, 'mgoingtodie, goingtodie...*

"Y'know," remarked the man who'd grabbed me in the garden, dragging me slightly from my daze as I waited to hear what he was going to say. "I really hate it when the parents don't even *tell* them."

"Really?" snorted the big man. "You prefer it when they go crazy with fear the moment they set eyes on you?"

"Huh."

They were talking like I wasn't even here. But then, if I really was an unRegistered child, I was nothing. Just spare parts. That's what the law said. Somewhere, a precious Registered child urgently needed something I had. Otherwise they wouldn't be taking me at this time in the evening. Making the Dismantlers do overtime... How much overtime? How long would it all... take? But what did that matter to me? I'd be unconscious the moment they got me in that Lab, and I'd never wake up again...

The shaking got worse. I could feel a sob trying to force its way out, and wrestled furiously with it, trying to hold it down. I wouldn't cry in front of these horrible men! I wouldn't. I *wouldn't.*

"What an idiot!" The muffled shout came from the

driver in the front. The other two guards leaned forward, peering through the windscreen, and I couldn't help looking too. We were approaching a bend in the road, and a car was coming up to it from the opposite direction, at tremendous speed. We could see the headlights flicking through the trees...

"Jeesh, he's asking for it..." The words had barely left the big man's mouth, when the oncoming car overshot the corner and smashed headlong into a tree, spun viciously, kept going, and slammed side-on into a rocky crag.

"Phewww," breathed the back door man, "that's got to have hur..."

He broke off as a massive explosion sent a shockwave smacking into us, making us swerve clear across the road and narrowly miss a tree ourselves.

Hydrogen tank...

As the driver, gasping, wrestled us into a straight line again, I blinked rapidly, the intense white of the explosion still hovering, ghost-like, in my vision. It all seemed unreal. Whoever was in that car was *dead.* Right before my eyes...

Clearly, I had no monopoly on death, this evening.

The driver said something, but I couldn't make it out. The noise of the explosion still rang in my ears.

The big man leaned forward and slid the Perspex back. "What?"

"I said, 'Should we stop?'"

Yes, stop! My heart leapt. Maybe, just maybe, I could...

"And do what? Give first aid? They're ash."

My heart sank again.

"We're not doing *anything?*" said the driver.

"Just call it in on the hands-free and let the emergency services deal with it..."

And suddenly, right then, I saw my chance. I'd have been terrified to do such a thing normally, but... Risk dying right now, or die for sure in a few hours time...

I snatched the big man's gun from his holster with my cuffed hands—"*Hey!*"—his big paw was reaching, but he was too late...

Because I'd pointed the gun straight through the open

Perspex window, at the back of the driver's head, and pulled the trigger.

K

Wow! What a bang! That worked so well! At any rate... well enough. The tree could have ruined everything, but it hit it so hard... I leaned against my protecting trunk, giddy with relief... or possibly the explosion.

Time for me to get out of here. A car was already approaching the scene of the crash. No doubt they'd stop and call the emergency services.

I couldn't help feeling sorry for all the people whose day would be ruined having to attend what they'd believe to be a fatal accident. But there was nothing I could do about that.

Anyway, it was Margo and my parents for whom my heart ached most.

Oh, they'd guess I wasn't dead. But getting the news, out of the blue like this, well, it would be just as though I were.

That was the whole point, of course.

Real tears would keep them safe.

JOE

The gun made no sound, but the driver slumped over the wheel, the car accelerating... both the guys in the back were yelling, but of course they couldn't do anything...

I dropped the nonLee pistol and buried my face in my legs, locking my arms around my knees as tightly as I could... wait for it...

The front of the car twisted and slid. The man's weight must be turning the wheel. Turning it far too fast... The right side of the car rose up, making my stomach lurch, and then it was rolling along the road, side over side... at least, that's how I interpreted the crazy motion... gravity kept flipping... the men grunting and gasping...

We must have gone right over about four times when the car suddenly stopped dead with the most appalling jolt.

My arms were almost jerked loose, and a couple of heavy limbs smacked into my back as the men were flung against their seatbelts.

A long, long moment of motionlessness, in which my head kept going round and round in a very unpleasant way, and the car suddenly toppled, crashing down onto its wheels, right side up again.

For several long seconds, I couldn't quite move. Even though I'd known we were about to crash, I still felt stunned. Reeling.

No, this was my chance. My only chance... *Move, Joe!*

I forced myself to sit up and look around. Back door guy was slumped in his seat, blood running down the side of his face. Unconscious? Big boss guy was stirring feebly, but no threat yet. A tree must've stopped the car, because the roof had been crushed right down across the middle, leaving no gap between it and the solid part under the Perspex window. I could just glimpse the driver slumped over the wheel still, but there was no way to get into the front...

Unbuckling the lap belt, I reached my hands across Unconscious Guy to open the door. But when I pulled the handle, nothing happened. Had the crash jammed it?

Gingerly, I leaned across Big Boss Guy and tried that one. *Oh no.* They were locked! And grilles covered the windows. Which meant... which meant I still couldn't get out! I'd still be sitting here when the police and ambulance arrived, and they'd probably take me straight on to the Facility! Or maybe they'd have to take me to hospital first and give me a clean bill of health, and *then* take me there...

No! No! Please, no!

I grabbed the door handle and yanked on it as hard as I could. Then I turned around and tried to get my feet against the other door, to kick it... It didn't move, but I kept trying. And trying.

Until hands closed around me.

"You little..." Big Boss Guy's voice was hoarse and furious. "You're not going *anywhere*, get that? *Get it?*"

He tried to drag me back into the middle seat, to buckle the lap belt around me again, but I struggled violently.

Help me! Help me! I was screaming it in my mind, but who to, I'd no idea.

I *had* to get the door open.

Somehow, I had to!

K

I peered from the undergrowth at the crashed car. My heart pounded like mad, half from the sprint through the forest to get here, and half at the thought that 'my' crash might have caused this one. But surely this car was driving along just fine right after the explosion, having safely correcting its swerve? Then, suddenly, it just flipped and went rolling down the road like a ball... until it also hit a tree.

Lord, please don't let this be my fault!

The worst thing was, I *could not* show myself. Too many lives would be lost if I did. I couldn't even call for help, since I had no phone. I wasn't sure what I actually could do; why I'd come tearing over here like this, except that I'd been driven by some immense sense of urgency...

Admittedly, the thought of just walking away and leaving injured people was almost unbearable... But how many members of the Salperton Underground would die if the Verralls were unmasked as Believers?

My agonized thoughts checked as I made it close enough to get a look at the vehicle. The hairs rose slightly on the back of my neck. Although it bore no logo, I knew what it was. Only one organization used normal cars with grilles over the back windows. And only for one purpose...

UnRegistered Child transportation.

Was there a kid trapped in there? A frightened kid?

Actually... I was even closer now... there seemed to be a fight going on in the back seat. Two figures were struggling together. One very big, one much smaller...

Lord, what do I do? What do I do?

But I knew: I simply could not walk away and leave a child to that fate. No matter what...

Lord, show me what to... Ah-ha, I see it!

Checking my balaclava and gloves were in place, I dropped to my hands and knees and crawled over to the vehicle. Gently, I eased the back door open a fraction. I slipped one hand into the crack and ran it up the edge of the door until I found the child lock. Snapped it into the 'off' position. They'd surely think the crash had done it...

Leaving the door ajar, merely resting in place, I crawled carefully back to the cover of the forest.

Lord, let it be enough...

JOE

I wasn't going back in that seat! I wasn't! He could kill me right here! Right here! I got in a punch to his nose, which already looked like it had connected with something during the crash, and he jerked away, swearing.

I scooted back into Unconscious Guy's lap, trying to put my back to the door, so I could kick the monster in the head... but when I pressed against the door, it swung open and I almost fell out...

Open? *Open!*

Yes, yes, yes...

Kicking against Big Boss Guy simply for purchase, now, I dived headfirst out into freedom...

"No, you don't!" A strong hand gripped my ankle...

I scrabbled at the ground with my cuffed hands, desperately seeking something to hold onto as he started to haul me back in... My free foot finally landed a good kick... where, I couldn't see, but his grip loosened. I kicked again... and suddenly I was falling to the ground...

Pushing up on my skinned palms, I staggered to my feet, booting the door into the guy as he tried to climb out, then I turned and stumbled into the forest.

Come on, Joe, run...

While he probably wasn't in much better shape than I was, his legs were a heck of a lot longer... But my head was steadying, and my legs were moving a little better. I held up my cuffed hands in front of me, trying to protect my eyes from branches and twigs...

At the top of the slope, I risked a look back, then paused...

In the light from the burning car, I could see Big Boss

Guy standing, bent over beside the crashed EGD car. It looked like he was busy being sick. Hah! No way would he be following me now. Well, not quite yet...

I'd just turned to make the most of his vomit-paralysis when a gloved hand slid over my mouth, and a strong arm immobilized mine.

"Shss..." someone whispered in my ear. "I'm not your enemy!"

Who... it must be the driver! How had he woken up already? I rammed my heel into the guy's shin as hard as I could and twisted free—started to run. He followed me.

He was fast, too. I thought nonLee made people feel awful when they woke up? How could he chase me like this?

And he was catching me! Panic exploded inside me. After all this, they were still going to drag me back there and kill me!

I ran on, but my legs were shaking and he was coming closer and closer.

"Stop!" he hissed. "For pity's sake stop! We're near the train tracks!"

He sounded younger than I remembered. Something in his words rang a subliminal alarm bell, but I was too tired to pay attention—and too desperate. He was close, so close...

Arms closed around me, hauled me in and held me so tightly I didn't think the shin thing was going to work a second time. "Stop!" His voice was so urgent now, I couldn't help listening. "There're train tracks ahead, do you understand? An electric rail. Please stop. I only want to help you."

"Help me?" My voice was thin. I wasn't sure how much more of this could I take. "Who... who are you?" Not the driver. In the sliver of moonlight filtering down into the trees, I could see he wore a balaclava. "Why would you help me?"

"Because I'm on the run from the EuroGov as well. I'm on my way out of the EuroBloc, in fact. And I'm guessing that's where you need to go. You can come with me, if you want to. I have the whole trip planned."

I stood there, almost leaning against him, my mind... swaying... with the shock and confusion of the evening. On the run... leaving the EuroBloc... I could go with him...

Where had he *come* from? Balaclava and... and gloves and all?

The car! The crashed car! He wanted everyone to think he was *dead!* He must really be against the EuroGov, then...

Could I trust him? No, no one could be *trusted*. But I didn't have much choice but to go with him. I mean, I was standing in the middle of the dark forest, with *nothing*, with my hands cuffed, without the first clue what to do or where to go. Of course I had to go with him.

"Yeah, I'd like to come."

Hang on... hang on... My stomach suddenly felt like a gripper locomotive with a broken cog... sliding back down, down, down the mountain, with nothing to hold it onto the track...

"Good," he was saying. "Because I'm worried about how you'd make out on your own..." His grip loosened, releasing me back to the mercy of the cold night air, but his hands traced the nasty 'bracelets' on my wrists. "Hmm, we'd better..."

"Wait..." My throat felt tight with fear, now. "Wait, I have a sister! Will they... will they take her... instead of me? Isn't that what they do?"

"Not in this case." He sounded very sure.

"Why not?" *Let it be true, oh let it be true...*

"Because you'd been taken into the EGD's custody, hadn't you? Your parents were no longer responsible for you—*they* were. It's just their tough luck they lost you. There's no way they can legally take your sister in your place. The moment they put you into that car, your sister was safe."

My heart was slowing again, but I was shaking hard with relief and leftover fear. "Are you... are you sure? You're not just... saying that to make me feel better?"

"I am absolutely certain." He sounded it, too. "I've studied all the vile Registration laws in considerable detail. They cannot touch your sister. There's absolutely nothing to stop you making a run for the border."

I swallowed, still shivering, though it was all relief, now. I believed him. He *knew.* Daisy was safe. I'd never even thought about that in the car, when I grabbed that pistol...

He tapped my handcuffs. "First thing tomorrow we'd better look for a farm workshop or something. Get those off. For now, let's get away from here. Far away."

"Right," I said nervously. Well, he sounded confident. And he did seem to have a plan. And some idea what to do.

But... I really wasn't sure why he'd revealed himself to me. Because I was quite certain he *didn't* need me. The opposite, in fact. But the one thing I *did* know was that *I didn't* know how to survive on my own. This guy was probably my only hope. And as soon as his common sense caught up with him and he realized what a liability I was going to be, he'd leave me...

Wait... what if I...? Well, that might force him to stay with me... or it might just make him kill me. But everything was going to be a gamble from now on, wasn't it?

Before I could chicken out, I raised my hand, not too fast, but not slow either, and grabbed the top of his balaclava... a split-second pause, to check just how violently he was going to react... He did nothing, so I yanked it off.

He was young. Way younger than his confidence had suggested. Eighteen, or close to it, no older. His hair was dark, his eyes almost invisible in the dimness.

He returned my searching gaze solemnly. "Well, now we really had better stick together like glue." A smile peeped. "Happy?"

Heat rushed to my face, as I realized he knew exactly why I'd just done that, and I found myself stammering. "Y...yes. Uh, my name's J...Joe, by the way."

Well, he seemed to have taken it all right. I suppose revealing himself to me, offering to help, making no attempt to stop me seeing his face, and *then* turning around and killing me would really make no sense at all.

He was smiling again. "Joe. Pleased to meet you. I'm..." He hesitated.

He was going to lie, wasn't he...?

"I'm... K."
Okay, not quite a lie. That was... surprisingly nice.
"K. Hi."

Present Time

*Somewhere in the French Department,
EuroBloc*

K

I ran. And ran. And ran. Joe's blood was soaking into my top and trickling down my chest and back, but it seemed like a million years before I finally dared to lay him on the ground.

His balaclava was gone, snatched away by some clutching twig, and his eyes glistened in the moonlight. No time to speak—or even check if there was life in them—soldiers' voices carried to my ears from not all that far away. I wouldn't have dared stop at all if I wasn't so scared that if I didn't do something about the bleeding, by the time it was actually 'safe' to take a break, Joe would definitely be dead.

Shielded—*please, Lord!*—behind what I thought was a thick bush, I dared—*had no choice but to*—pull out my red torch and shine it at Joe. My chest knotted up as I took in the extent of the wetness that'd spread up the front of his jacket and halfway down his trousers. Oh God, should I have stopped sooner? But the soldiers had been right on my *heels...*

I pulled up his clothes as quickly as I could and got a look at last. The hole in his back was tiny, just off centre to the left of his spine, but the exit wound on the other side of his abdomen was the size of a small child's fist. My stomach knotted up, making my entire upper torso rigid with shock and dread. Joe needed a doctor. No, he *needed* a fully equipped hospital emergency department... *Now.* Or fifteen minutes ago...

A twig snapped somewhere behind us... Quickly, I shed the rucksack, slipped off my jacket, rolled it into a makeshift bandage and tied it around Joe's body. Yanking my belt out of its loops, I buckled it around for good measure, trying to get the jacket as tight as possible.

Finally, pocketing the torch and hauling the rucksack back on again, I managed to breathe a few words: "It's okay, Joe, I got a bandage on, but we've got to move..." As I hefted Joe back up over my shoulder, his faint whimper of pain was music to my ears.

Dead boys didn't whimper.

JOE

Shadowy trees flashed by upside down in the dim moonlight, trees and bushes and unidentified twisting shapes... Sometimes branches yanked my hair or managed to catch my cheeks. I felt dizzy and disorientated. My mind seemed to be working ever so slowly through a haze of pain and... and... *haze.*

I'd been shot. I was sure of that much.

K was carrying me. That seemed fairly clear as well.

Other questions gradually floated up. How badly was I hurt? How long would K bother to carry me for? What would happen when he put me down and left me?

I wasn't sure I wanted to know the answer to those questions... But my mind insisted on slowly but surely grinding out the answers. When he left me, I would die alone on the forest floor. Or the soldiers would find me. What would *they* do? Drive me straight to the nearest Facility so my undamaged organs wouldn't go to waste? Horrendous as the first fate seemed, I preferred it to the second...

Maybe he *wouldn't* leave me...

And maybe we were on the moon. What was *I* to him, *really?* When the soldiers got too close, or he got too tired, or... or if it became clear I could no longer go on... he'd put me down. Make some excuse, maybe, and slip away, leaving me to my fate. Just as my parents had done. Just as God had done. I knew real love didn't exist, the lesson had been too agonizing to forget.

Could I go on? Hard to tell, hanging here like this. But from the horrible, leaden dullness that gripped my entire body, I'd a nasty feeling going on under my own steam was no longer an option. My life was entirely in K's hands. It'd *kind of* been ever since he found me, but now it was *literally* so.

The only question was whether he'd try harder to save me than Mum and Dad had done...

My heart ached in a way that had nothing to do with the pain burning through my belly. I'd take the bullet pain, any day...

Why didn't you even try?

Why did you lie?

This 'God the Father' K talked about was just like my real dad, too. All this stuff about him loving me, and then he let me get shot like this...

But as I hung there, limply, and K ran on and on—his shoulders heaving as he panted under my weight—stuff that K had said filtered slowly back into my mind, rolling around like water in the bilges of a boat.

...People do evil things, not God...

...God simply permits them to...

...Because otherwise we'd just be his puppets...

"Would you like to be a puppet, Joe?" K had asked me. Again I heard my vehement, "No!"

Was this the price of that 'No'?

I was losing track of time. The sky was lightening. My heart leapt at the thought of *dawn*... of being free of this darkness, of being able to see. But... if we could see, we could be seen. Maybe light wasn't good after all...

K was muttering something to himself as he slogged up a steep rocky slope. He wasn't running now. His shoulder was no longer hot under me, despite hours of exertion. He must be whacked. He'd been whispering prayers for miles?... hours?... millennia?... but the rhythm of his murmurings had changed. He was debating with himself...

Whether to leave me?

He slipped behind some bushes and... *yeowwww—ow— oww*... I barely bit back a scream as he laid me on the ground...

"Sorry," he whispered, "I'm sorry, Joe! It's okay, you're down! Just lie still, I'm going to look for a hiding place. This rocky area looks promising. Don't make a sound, I'll be back soon."

And he was gone.

It felt like another bullet had just slammed right through my heart. The pain was terrible.

He wasn't coming back, was he? He was too exhausted to carry me any further, so he'd told me a comforting lie to make me feel better—just like Mum and Dad did—and he'd split...

Hot tears spilled from my eyes. Anger surged inside me,

anger at *me*. I'd known better than to trust anyone, surely, but I *had*—or I wouldn't be crying like this. Well, I didn't *need* K! I'd take care of myself...

But when I tried to roll onto my front, ready to get to my feet... I couldn't. Pain stabbed my abdomen, but I barely managed to get one shoulder off the ground. My body felt like a limp rag. I flopped back, and the question I'd been trying to avoid stormed squarely into my mind.

Am I going to die?

I tried to lift my head enough to look down the length of myself... *Argh*, it felt like a concrete railway sleeper attached to my neck, so *heavy*... somehow, somehow, I lifted it until my chin pressed to my chest, and managed to focus. Some rolled up clothing—K's jacket?—was strapped around me, gleaming damply in the faint light. Was that... dew?

It wasn't dew. The jacket was soaked with my blood. My head thudded back onto the ground as my strength ran out. So *much* blood...

How much more could I lose? K clearly didn't think he could do anything for me. The cold feeling that gripped my belly had nothing to do with the wound... or everything to do with it.

Yes, whispered a helpful/unhelpful little voice in my mind. *You are going to die. Here on the ground. Alone. K left you to die. Alone.*

I was crying again. Crying like a baby, but I couldn't stop. My mind had fragmented into a million agonizing shards of fear and pain and hurt. I just retained the sense to keep as quiet as possible. If it was all over, I'd rather die quickly—comparatively quickly—here in the forest, free, than be kept just alive enough, just long enough, to die on a cold gurney, my body pillaged and scattered.

But I couldn't stop sobbing. Pain and weakness robbed me of all control. I didn't want to die. But even more, I didn't want to be unloved. Alone and unloved and undefended and... unwanted. Or... not wanted *enough*, just up until I needed something, *really really* needed something.

My parents didn't want me enough, nor did K.

My brain made a few feeble attempts to defend K, asking if I wanted him to die too, if I wanted his family to die—what would be the point of that?—but I couldn't stop the tears.

He didn't have to *lie*. He could have just said *Sorry, but I have to go; I hope you understand.* I'd probably still be crying, but it wouldn't be quite so bad...

A rustling in the bushes... then a hand settled on my shoulder.

"Hey, Joe, shhh, shhh. Is the pain really bad?" K. It was *K.* "Shhh, it's okay, I've found quite a good place to hide. As soon as I get you in there, I can give you some painkillers, okay? Can you be brave for just another few minutes?"

Brave? My tears had choked off mid-sob, I was that shocked to see him again, but I couldn't understand how he could call me brave just now...

"You came back..." I said stupidly.

His eyes narrowed as he looked down at me. It was getting a lot lighter, now... "Of course. I'm really sorry, Joe, I thought you heard what I said before I left you. I was just looking for somewhere for us to hole up. Come on, up we go..."

Owwwwwwww...

He hadn't thrown me over his shoulder again, thank goodness—though his rucksack was missing—but simply hefted me into his arms. By the time the pain had died down enough for my vision to clear, he was wriggling through some rock formations and hanging undergrowth and laying me down in a narrow crack in the cliff face...

Owwwwwww...

When I opened my eyes again, K was gone. My heart crashed right back to the ground. He'd hidden me, and *then* he'd left...

But... no, there he was, at the entrance, on hands and knees, crawling backwards into the crack, peering closely at the ground. Oh, getting rid of tracks. He scrambled over to me without bothering to stand again and brushed my hair out of my eyes in that gentle way I often objected to—'*I'm not a baby!*'—though right now I couldn't think why I'd ever complained. His smile was warm... but strained.

"Right, let's get you fixed up a bit better. Painkillers first." He didn't manage to sound quite confident enough to fool me.

He unfastened his rucksack, already stowed further back in the crack, and dug out the 'magic bag'—his first aid kit. Supporting my head carefully, he fed me at least ten pills, which must be about eight more than it said on the packet. I guess he knew it was safe. Or did it... simply not matter anymore?

The terror monster began to chomp up my insides again. "K?" I whispered.

"Yes, Joe?"

"Please don't leave me..." The words squeezed out, cowardly and selfish, and quite unstoppable.

He pillowed my head in his lap and stroked my hair back again. "Of course I'm not going to leave you, Joe." He sounded totally... dismissive... of the idea, as though I'd just suggested jumping off a cliff would be a wise and sensible course of action. "Just lie still and let those pills work. Then I can change your bandage without hurting you."

"Is there... is there any point?" It came out half a sob.

"Any point?" K sounded closed, almost wary.

"Changing it..." There was no almost about the sob this time. "I'm... I'm going to die, aren't I?"

K was silent for far too long. "If the soldiers miss us," he said at last, "which I think they're likely to do..."

"Won't they bring dogs?"

"I walked along several streams. I think I lost them quite well. But they'll probably walk through here in a line, searching. I don't think they'll find this place, and once they've gone, I'm going to carry you down to the nearest town and take you to a doctor; get you put to rights."

"Doctor'll turn us in."

"They might not. I don't think we have any choice, anyway."

For a few minutes, I was happy to lie there, enjoying this fantasy of a doctor and waiting for the pills to act. But I had too great a craving for the truth, these days.

"K?"

"Hmm?"

"How far is the town?"

"I'm... not sure."

That didn't matter either, did it?

"K?"

"Hmm?"

"Am I going to die?"

K

Joe's quiet persistence wrenched at my own unpierced insides.

"I'm not a doctor, Joe. I have no medical training. But..." Joe hadn't stopped with the comforting, best possible case scenario. That meant he really did want to know. I took a deep breath, as though that would help somehow. "Yes. I think so."

Joe squeezed his eyes closed. He sniffed slightly but didn't break down again. His courage tore up my insides some more.

"I'm sorry," I whispered. "I'm *so sorry*, Joe..."

His eyes opened again and stared at me, bleak and pain-filled. "It wasn't your fault," he whispered back. "At least you *tried* to save me!"

I had no answer to that. How deeply his parent's failure had hurt him—and no wonder—but I had no idea how to heal that hurt, other than with love. And if he could only forgive them, of course...

But I'd failed him too. From the first, I'd felt as though he'd been given to me to look after, to protect. And I'd failed. I'd failed as badly as it was possible to fail. Doctor I might not be, but I'd no real doubt he was going to die. Quite honestly, I was surprised he was still alive.

WHY, Lord?

I couldn't hold back the silent cry, even though I knew *why*. Another human being, a soldier in the pay of the EuroGov, had somehow brought himself to line up his sights on a fleeing child and pull a trigger. Almost beyond comprehension, but that was *why*.

And I'd been *trying* to shield Joe, I'd *tried*...

Unless... unless, horrendous thought, unless the soldier wasn't aiming at Joe at all. Unless he was aiming at *me* and simply *missed*. Maybe not even an accidental miss. Maybe he hadn't particularly wanted to shoot *me* either, and it was all more a tragic accident than anything... Maybe he'd been beyond horrified when he saw Joe fall. Maybe, like me, he would bear the guilt of this night until the day he died...

Who knew?

The Lord. Not me.

The Lord knew everything.

My heart felt as though it was clenched up, like a fist, so tight the sinews ought to crack. I wanted to scream out my pain and grief and fear, to pound on the rocky walls until my hands bled—my *useless* hands that had totally failed to save Joe, that could do nothing, nothing for him now...

Somehow, I managed to simply stroke his fair hair, gently, soothingly. A wordless reassurance—*I'm here, Joe, I'm here...* Much use I was.

Why did love have to hurt so much? Why did we stupid humans *let* ourselves love? But with that thought came the memory of that hour walking through the forest, the better part of two weeks ago. Well away from any roads or built-up areas, with a week's food on my back, the last of the clothes and things Joe had needed successfully—and discreetly—acquired, and Joe even beginning to manage a full day's walking more easily, I'd felt unusually calm that afternoon. For the first time since I'd 'died' on that road outside Salperton, I'd achieved a really prayerful state of mind.

And I'd felt God's love. Not the first time, but I'd rarely felt it so strongly or so persistently.

And I'd also felt his love for *Joe*. His burning, overwhelming, pouring torrent, volcanic-eruption... no, no words could express it. Oh, *how* he loved us. How he loved Joe.

And even then, that Eternal Mind, love itself, had known...

JOE

Shivering... shivering so hard, now. *Cold... so cold...*

K was moving around... oh, digging my trusty foil blanket out. He examined the bandage closely but finished tucking the blanket over me without changing it. I guess he didn't have anything better or couldn't see the point hurting me by messing with it. I tried to return his smile but my head felt heavy. Swimming. Maybe it was all those pain-killers. It didn't seem to hurt quite as much now, though whether that was simply because I was lying still...

"This crack gets even smaller further in," K was telling me. "It would be warmer, but the walls turn into dirt back there and they don't look too stable, so I think we'd better stay put."

The looming walls around us were great slabs of rock, framing a sliver of dull dawn-grey sky... I stared up at them with my slow thoughts. From down here, they looked like they were about to topple in and crush me. It wouldn't really matter if they did...

Not to me.

But I didn't want K to die. I couldn't believe he was still here. He was risking his life by staying with me... and his family's lives. But the thought of lying here, alone, waiting...

But K didn't have to die. Whereas I was done for anyway... He was being so... what's the word... selfless. And I was being incredibly self*ish*.

"K?" I said at last, in a small voice.

"Umhum?" K was starting to shiver as well. He must've been chilling fast, now he'd stopped running.

"Just... just give me something from your magic bag to make me sleep and... and leave me."

K made no move to reach for the first aid kit, and the selfish part of my heart leapt in desperate hope. Instead, he shifted my head onto my rucksack, settled himself beside me and tucked the blanket around himself too. "I'm not going anywhere, Joe."

"But your family..."

"Would understand. That I couldn't possibly leave my little brother. Yeah, I've felt like you were my little brother for ages, so I might as well make it official by saying it. Do you mind?"

Mind? My brain had gummed up completely. He was saying he'd *adopted* me? "Does... does that make it official?" I stuttered at last. "Just saying it?"

45

"Well, not in the eyes of the EuroGov, perhaps, but who cares about them. Before God, I'm sure it's good. So *our* sister would understand that I couldn't possibly leave you. She would *totally* understand."

"How do you know?"

"Because she would never in a million years leave you either. Even if you *weren't* her little brother."

"I wish I could meet her," I whispered, though talking was getting very tiring. Everything was getting tiring.

K spoke so softly I almost didn't hear him. "Someday, I hope you will."

I frowned up at the rock walls. He'd said himself that I was going to die. How would I ever meet his... oh, he was talking about the afterlife-thing, wasn't he?

I thought about the afterlife-thing for a few minutes. Or possibly hours. I couldn't tell any more. K had told me that— according to him and his stream of the religious underground—you could have a nice afterlife if you got adopted by God in a special ritual... a sacrament, K called it. Not *just* a ritual, he'd explained, because it's not only a symbol of something, it actually *does* that thing. In some very mysterious—and rather cool—way...

If you never got adopted, your afterlife was a *whole* lot less certain, depending on all sorts of factors like whether you'd ever been offered the ritual... sacrament... or not, whether you really understood what you were being offered if you'd rejected it, and so on and so on. I'd turned him down flat when he offered it to *me*, though. The thought of another father to betray me had turned my stomach.

But... K *hadn't* betrayed me. K wasn't going to leave me, even if it cost him his life and those of everyone he loved. What if this other Father was like *K*, not like my dad? Wouldn't it be nice to be His son?

And let's face it: the nice afterlife part certainly looked very attractive right now...

That wasn't a good enough reason, though, was it...? I mean, just wanting to get something out of it...

I could hear myself, a week or so back, demanding an answer from K: "Is *that* why you want to become a priest?

To make sure you have a really, *really* nice afterlife?" I'd been thinking about it for days, ever since he told me what he hoped to do with his life, trying to figure out why he would *ever* risk such a nightmarish death... The only answer I'd come up with was that he thought he was going to get something *really, really, really* good out of it... eventually.

K had looked astonished, though. "You don't get a... a *better* afterlife, just because you're a priest," he'd told me. "Priests aren't any holier than anyone else, though goodness knows if anyone should work hard at it, it's them."

I'd been back to square one, and pretty frustrated to find myself there. "Then *why*? Why do it! Aren't you... *scared?*"

"No," K had said, his face grim. "I'm *terrified.*"

"Then why? Are you... are you just plain crazy?"

K had—almost—smiled, at that. "I hope not. It's just... well, I'm not sure how to explain it... It's like, my whole life, someone I love, and who loves me more than anything in the universe, has been calling out to me asking me to help with something. Calling and calling and calling to me. And... well, for some years I *did* try to ignore Him. Because I was so scared. I pretended I couldn't hear Him at all. But I *could. Help me,* He was saying. *Help me with this task I have for you. Help your brothers and sisters. Come to Me.* How can you ignore someone who loves you as much as He loves me? And you? And everyone?

"Well, you *can* do it for a while, or I could, but I couldn't keep it up. It was ruining my relationship with Him. Being so sure, deep down, what He was asking, and refusing to do it. So I... I stopped pretending I couldn't hear Him, and ran towards Him instead. And perhaps I'll be with Him—in person, as it were—sooner than if I'd gone on ignoring Him. But no pain is worse than a lifetime of guilt and grief and... and sundering... because I ignored the person I love the most when He called out and begged me to come to Him."

His words had struck me so deeply at the time. It felt like K and God were like my parents and me. Only *I'd* called and they hadn't run to *me.* God was luckier than me, to have K.

But what if... what if God wasn't just calling to K? What if He was calling to me too? What if He'd sent me K, K who hadn't abandoned me, K who kept telling me God loved me, because... because *I* wasn't listening?

Had I ever heard... something... that could be God? I tried to think, but it was too hard. I guess I'd never noticed, so God got bored of waiting and sent K...

I tried to focus on K's face, there beside me. My vision blurred... cleared... blurred again... Finally he came into focus properly. He had his eyes closed, but his lips moved slightly. Praying?

When his eyes opened, focusing on me effortlessly, he looked... tense. Anxious. Like he was about to do something very important. He took a deep breath and opened his mouth...

"Yes," I said. 'Cos I suddenly felt very sure.

He blinked. "Yes?"

"Yes, please. Baptize me."

Relief and... joy... flooded his face. "You mean it?"

"Yes. Quickly..." Now I'd decided I did want it after all, I didn't want to peg it before I got it.

Even breathing was getting to be very hard work...

K

"Joseph Verrall Whitelow, I baptize you in the name of the Father, and of the Son, and of the Holy Spirit..."

Feeling more than a touch of... of reverse déjà vu?... I carefully trickled water from the bottle over Joe's forehead, three times, traced a cross there, then gently blotted the water out of his tightly closed eyes with my sleeve. "There, all done. Simple, you see. But God is now your Father, the Lord Jesus is your Brother, the Holy Spirit is... well, *something like* your Sister, and Mother Mary is your mother. Spiritually. Your physical mother and father are still your... your earthly parents, of course."

Joe's face tightened at the mention of his useless mum and dad. I tried to censor that judgmental thought, removing the 'useless', but I knew my heart wasn't entirely in the correction.

Would my mum and dad flee with Margo? If her Math didn't improve, these next three years? Bane certainly would. *If* she told him... And fat chance of that, when it would put him at risk...

But she'd be fine. She was confident...

I choked off that cycle of worry and focused on Joe again. It was full light outside and sunlight streamed down into the crack, which only allowed me to see just how grey and awful his face looked. His lips were bluish and permanently parted as he drew in slow, strained breaths.

Pain tried to wring my insides out at the sight of him like this.

Oh Lord... oh Lord, give me strength. Help me to be strong for him. Don't let me fall apart...

"All the saints and all other Believers are your brothers and sisters, as well," I went on, somehow keeping my voice steady. "So you're my brother twice over, now."

Despite the fact he was clearly fighting for his life with every breath, Joe looked... calmer. "You should go," he whispered. "I don't want you to die too."

I slipped my arms around him and held him close. "I'm not going anywhere," I whispered back. "Not until you're safely home. So there's no point going on about it." But a few tears escaped at last—I tried to draw back but one splashed onto Joe's face.

"K? Are you... crying?"

"Maybe a little," I admitted.

"Why?"

"*Why?*"

"I mean, if you really think I'm going somewhere wonderful...?"

Goodness, even lying there half-dead, the kid asked such perceptive questions. It did nothing to stop the tears, though, since it simply reminded me of all the things I loved about him. "I'm not crying *for* you, Joe. I'm crying for *me*, because I'm going to miss you *such* a lot. These are very selfish tears, I'm afraid."

"Oh."

"And my name isn't K. It's Kyle. Kyle Verrall."

JOE

Verrall... He'd used that name when he baptized me. I'd assumed it was a special religious name, like Joseph—'cos it just said plain old 'Joe' on my birth certificate. But it wasn't. It was *his* name. I was, like, *officially* his brother...

And my brother's name is Kyle Verrall.

Despite the coldness that seemed to have settled into every bone in my body, that gave me a nice warm feeling. Not a physical one, no doubt, but who cared.

I knew that his name was the greatest gift he could give me—well, other than the Baptism-thing, I suppose—since, as I was still alive—just about—it meant that if soldiers turned up, even if *he* managed to flee, they could try to beat it out of me. I hoped I wouldn't tell them. I really, really hoped I wouldn't. I also really hoped I wouldn't be tested on that.

I'd always liked to think of myself as brave, but it'd taken one of those conversations with K—Kyle—a week or so back to make me face up to the fact that I wasn't perhaps as brave as I'd always prided myself on being.

"Were you ever bullied at school?" K had asked me.

I'd shrugged. "Not really. I wasn't hyper-cool or anything, but I wasn't one of *those* kids, either. The ones everyone picked on. I should've been, of course, being Dead Meat. But my parents kept it secret."

But they could have kept it secret from everyone *else* and still told *me...* My heart ached all over again, at the thought of their lies.

"Did you feel sorry for those kids?" K had gone on.

"Yeah, of course. It sucked to be them."

"So you stood up for them, then?"

"Stood up for them?" My stomach had given a really uncomfortable sort of sideways lurch, at that. "What... what do you mean?"

"Well, you clearly felt sorry for them. I just thought you might have tried to stop the bullies, sometimes."

"Well, I mean, sorry, yes, but..." I'd been floundering by then. "I mean, they're *those* kids. You don't... stand up for them. I mean, you'll end up *one of them*, that way."

"I never did."

I'd eyed K, my face hot and my insides churning with

shame and embarrassment. "You... used to stand up for them?"

"Well, sometimes I chickened out, especially when I was younger. But yes, when I could."

"Well... well... you're really big and... and strong... and... I'm not. Really big. Or strong. I'm quite little for my age, aren't I? How could I stand up to the bullies? They were some of the biggest boys in my age group. Strong. Mean. How could I possibly take them on?"

"So you think it's okay to stand back and let something bad happen if you don't feel you're strong enough to stop it? If the people doing it are very much stronger and more powerful than you are?"

"Well... not *okay*... I didn't say that. *Exactly*. But... but you can only do what you can do, you know? Are you... are you calling me a coward?" I'd felt hot inside, right down into my belly, at the thought that K considered me a coward.

"No, I'm not calling you a coward," K had said, his tone still friendly—relief had filled me at that. "I'm just saying that sometimes people are paralyzed in the face of something overwhelmingly stronger than themselves. And no, it's not really okay. But it is *understandable*. Do you see what I mean?"

Not really, K, I'd thought to myself. Because I'd a nasty feeling what he was really saying was only that he wasn't going to *call* me a coward, and I didn't want to accept that.

"I just mean we should try not to judge people too harshly," he'd added, when I didn't reply. "We *all* do things— or *don't* do things—out of weakness even when we really, really, really *want* to do them with all our heart. It's always best to forgive weakness like that. Well, it's always best to forgive, period..."

KYLE

"So I guess you're not going to swear to avenge me, then..." murmured Joe, as though continuing a conversation I wasn't aware we'd been having.

I brushed the hair back from his forehead again. "Would you even... want me to?"

He frowned... his lips moved slowly, but he was talking to himself... "What would that even mean... kill the soldier, I guess... If Kyle killed the soldier... *he wouldn't*... but if he did... soldier would be dead. Soldier's parents would be upset, I guess, if they liked him... Lives ruined, maybe... I'd still be totally dead... wouldn't achieve much..."

Joe's eyes moved back towards me, though he seemed to be having trouble focusing. But he was clearly speaking to me again. "No. I don't think it would help."

"That's all right, then."

"Soldier's... not really the problem..." murmured Joe.

"No, he's not. But I will promise you this, Joe. If I ever get a chance to do something, anything—anything moral—to bring down the EuroBloc Genetics Department, I'll do it. I promise you. Even if it costs me my life."

But Joe's eyes widened in distress. "No... not *your* life... You have to live... *No*..."

I hugged him tight and tried to soothe him. "Of course, Joe. I'll be very careful. It's okay. Shhh. Don't you worry about me..."

He calmed again, but I carried on stroking his hair, on and on.

Lord, please help me. Please give me the words to help him understand... Please, Lord. Quickly!

JOE
I couldn't seem to make out K's face any more, but I could feel him, holding me. It made me feel very safe. I relaxed again. It was bizarre that a little water from our drinking bottle and a few words from K and 'yes' a couple of times from me could make me feel so much better about everything, but I just didn't feel so scared any more. I really trusted K's judgment, and he thought God was real and that God was now my Father, so I believed it too.

It was odd having a new family. An invisible, holy family. No doubt they were going to be visible to me pretty soon, now... What would my old family have thought?

I'd never even known my parents' views on God. We'd never talked about it. I guess they'd never have dared, for fear of the EuroGov. Like me and the bullies...

Like...

Like me and the bullies.

Like...

Oh. My. Freaking. Goodness.

I'd thought that conversation was about *me*. But it wasn't about *me* at all, was it? It was about my *parents!* In that conversation, *I* was 'those kids', my parents were 'me', too afraid to help, and the EGD, *they* were 'the bullies'. How could it take me this long to figure that out?

K had been trying to make me understand. How my parents felt. Why they failed me like that. He hadn't pretended it was okay. But he had been trying to get me to *understand*.

Perhaps I did, now. Again I saw my mum's face as they dragged me away... My dad sitting motionless in that chair, his face that ghastly mask...

No, I still didn't understand how they felt. Because how I'd felt when I'd failed to stand up to a few bullies to help someone I didn't even know very well could never compare with how they must have felt... How they would feel for the rest of their lives...

Wishing for revenge on *them* would be beyond pointless.

KYLE

"K?" Joe's voice was so faint, now.

I knew he wasn't rejecting my real name, he was simply too weak now to remember that my name just changed...

"Yes, Joe?"

"Can you do something for me?"

"What?" I asked gently.

"When you get to Vatican State, will you write to my parents? Tell them it's okay and that I forgive them? Well... it's not okay, but I do forgive them... Will you?"

"Of course, Joe. I promise." My heart swooped upwards, soaring in relief. I'd been praying and praying and God hadn't been giving me any words... because he knew Joe was in the process of figuring it out for himself. *Thank you, Lord!*

"Tell me their address."

Joe blinked, though he didn't really seem to be focusing on anything at all, now. When I moved a hand in front of his eyes, he didn't react. His body was shutting down all non-essentials as it fought its losing battle.

"Um... Mr. and Mrs. Whitelow... Bob and Karen Whitelow, that is... uh... um... um... *oh!*"

Joe was clearly struggling to remember and starting to freak out... "Shhhh, shhh, Joe, it's okay. Just take your time. Mr. and Mrs. Whitelow..." I recited soothingly. "Take your time..." I wasn't sure he *had* time, but panicking would only make it worse...

Joe lay quietly for a few minutes, his breathing a little slower. Finally, he recited the address all the way through.

I recited it back to him. "I'll write to them, Joe. I promise. I'll tell them."

"Good," he whispered. "And... and tell Daisy I love her..."

"I will. I promise." How clearly I remembered the anguish in his voice that night we met, as he asked me if his sister was safe. I'm not sure he wouldn't have given himself up, if I hadn't been able to assure him of her safety...

Joe's hand twitched urgently, struggling to reach out, and his voice had gone thin and frightened. "K? K, are you still there?"

I slipped the hand of the arm I had around his shoulders over his, gripping tight, leaving my other hand free to go on stroking his hair, and I held him as close as I could. "I'm still here, Joe. I'm still here. I'm not going anywhere. I'm here, and God's here. Your new Father. Or your original Father, depending on how you look at it. He's here. He loves you so much. He's loved you since the beginning of creation. He's really looking forward to having you with Him..."

JOE

K was still there. I could feel him. He was talking to me, nice things, but I couldn't take it in any more. Concentrating was... was just too hard. His words faded to a gentle murmur, like a fuzzy, friendly bee was buzzing lovingly in my ear.

I was loved.

I was wanted.

I was so completely wrapped up in K's love that it took me a while to realize maybe it wasn't just *his* love. Maybe it was my mysterious new Father's love as well. Maybe my whole new family were around me, loving me, and that was why I felt such happiness.

I wanted to tell K about it, but I wasn't sure how to speak. I couldn't seem to find my mouth; it was so far away, so very far away...

Maybe... maybe K already knew.

Maybe this was what he'd been trying to tell me.

My Father loved me. And wanted me.

And held me.

And held...

Held...

Me...

KYLE

Joe wasn't responding any more. His breathing had gone funny, long, slow, gasping breaths that arched his back. I didn't stop talking, though. I talked softly, on and on, right in his ear, telling him about heaven, telling him how much God loved him, how much I loved him...

Even when the gasping stopped and he lay still, I went on talking to him. Uncle Peter had once told me that he would speak to the dying for at least several minutes after all their vital signs had stopped. Hearing was the last sense to go, so they said, and he didn't want them to be plunged into lonely silence at the very last. The thought of Joe being plunged into silence...

I couldn't bring myself to stop at all. Only a branch breaking out in the forest finally brought my lips snapping together.

More crashing sounds. A murmur of grumpy voices...

Soldiers.

Finally.

I clutched Joe, clung to him, even though I knew I

couldn't protect him now, or he me, and I waited. Waited to see whether Margo and my parents would die for a relative they'd never even meet. Not in this life. I'd never even considered leaving Joe, and I knew they wouldn't have expected me to, but still, there was a lot at stake, far more than just my insignificant life...

Oh, Joe... Pray for us... Perhaps *he could* protect *me*, now...

The soldiers passed quickly. When they'd gone, I closed Joe's sightless eyes, and then I couldn't hold back the tears any longer. I clung to Joe some more and sobbed out my anguish. My guilt. I knew he was in a better place now. I knew he wouldn't regret his lost life now he stood in the presence of God. But life was still a precious gift, and his had been snatched from him so cruelly.

And I'd failed to prevent it.

I managed not to howl or scream like I wanted to. Good thing too, since more crashing around in the distance finally dried up my tears. For over three hours, I lay motionless beside my little brother, listening to the occasional sounds of passing—and increasingly bored—searchers and praying like crazy.

Finally, silence—or normal forest sounds—fell over everything again. I crept out and listened, and looked. When finally ready to stake my life on there being no one around, I returned to Joe.

Though I hated doing it, I searched his pockets, his backpack, absolutely everywhere, for anything that might give away even the slightest clue about my identity. Then, crawling, I dragged him as far into the crack as I could, right to the back. He *was* small for his age. Thank God for that, or I couldn't have carried him so far last night.

I propped his backpack under his feet, not his head—he'd have gotten the joke, though I don't think he'd realized that I understood exactly why he always claimed my legs made a more comfortable pillow. Wrapping his foil blanket around him as a silvery shroud—fit for a beloved child of God—I knelt beside him for a few more long minutes, trying to tear myself away. Trying not to let the grief and guilt tear me apart.

Are you... are you trying to make sure I'll be happy to come to you, Lord? The very Kyle-centric thought floated through my mind. Silly. And no offense to Joe, it would take more than this to make me relish the prospect of Full Conscious Dismantlement...

But...

I was the *worst, lousiest* excuse for a big brother ever. I mean, what sort of big brother lets their little bro get killed, for pity's sake?

At least... at least I could be pretty jolly sure Joe was with God, and happy there. He'd looked so peaceful at the end, a smile on his face... It was just slack and empty and dead now, but I'd never forget his happy little smile...

How could I have let this happen? Unstoppably, I found myself running through my every decision and action, hunting for the fatal error that had brought about Joe's death... but I couldn't find it. Every choice I'd made, I would make again, if only I did not know...

I struggled to force the guilty thoughts back. After all, before the end of his short life, Joe had come to know God and, though I wasn't sure he'd had time to properly comprehend it, I was pretty sure he'd come to love him too. And that was the ultimate purpose of life, right? He could have lived another hundred years, driven a thousand trains, but if he'd not achieved that, his life would've been totally wasted...

I mean, his slipping away into God's loving embrace here today was only a tragedy in a worldly sense. Spiritually... spiritually, it was his *triumph.* I had to hold onto that truth; refuse to let the guilt devour me. I had done everything I could, and in the eternal equation, it had been enough.

Just not in the physical one... *Joe, I'm so sorry...* I *knew* he was okay—more than okay—but... just now all I wanted was my little brother back.

So mostly I was just feeling sorry for *myself,* wasn't I? *Selfish tears,* no lie, that.

"Goodbye, little bro," I whispered, at last. Placing a kiss on his cold forehead, I tucked the blanket over his head and fetched a sturdy branch.

It took more effort working on the earth walls than I expected, but finally they gave way. I ran for it, but the landslide swallowed me up, and for several long, choking, crushing, roaring, head over heels moments of turmoil and terror I thought I was joining Joe, for certain.

But when the dirt and dust settled, I found that my head and upper body were free of the dirt. I'd reached the stone-sided section again—almost. Digging myself out uninjured, I knelt to pray for a few minutes in front of what was really a very fine tomb indeed, on the scale of some ancient barrow or something—Joe would have appreciated that intriguing comparison. Best of all, from my point of view and that of my family, it was quite invisible from outside. Hopefully the EuroGov would never find him. Ever.

I might never find the place again, either, and that wasn't such a happy thought. But I knew the life expectancy of an underground priest in a EuroBloc parish, so if I did indeed have a vocation, I was unlikely to ever be back here looking. I'd probably be speaking to Joe face-to-face inside a decade.

So, finally, shouldering my backpack, I checked one last time for any trace of our presence and went on my way. Alone.

Although I was trying to stay alert, in case there were any stray searchers still around, I couldn't stop the tears trickling down my face as I walked. *Big and strong, Joe? Is that really how you saw me? Not so much, huh?* I'd lost plenty of people I knew—most of the assistant priests and religious sisters who'd ever come to Salperton, for starters. But nothing had hurt like this. Even though I'd only known him three weeks, Joe really was my little brother.

This was all the EGD's fault. That vilest of institutions. They would kill my sister, if she didn't make the grade, and they'd as good as killed Joe.

Their ideology is evil. Pure evil, Lord.

I'd meant what I'd said to Joe. If I ever got a chance to do something to bring them down, I'd do it, whatever the risk. If only someone *could* bring them down...

Weird. Why did my sister suddenly come into my mind, in a way that suggested the Holy Spirit's agency?

Surely *Margo* couldn't bring down the EGD, could she? My little sister? Very eloquent, and passionate, certainly, and, to be honest, able to outshoot Bane or myself with Bane's air rifle, but still. How could she? Surely *Bane* was the one people might follow, one day, if he ever calmed down enough and used his head instead of charging in without thinking about the risks?

But... maybe if Margo *was* going to do something to fight the EGD, it meant she *was* going to pass her Sorting! My heart tried to lift, but... the thought simply rang false.

So, what are you saying, Lord? Margo's going to fail her Sorting, yet somehow bring down the EGD? How could that happen?

I suppose the universe happened too, and that's pretty hard to believe. You are God, after all. But no doubt I'm just misunderstanding this one.

I mean, could Margaret Verrall really bring down the EuroGov?

But as I carried on walking and crying, five more words popped into my head:

Oh ye of little faith.

DON'T MISS BOOK 1

I AM MARGARET

In Margo's world, if you don't pass your Sorting at 18 you are recycled.

Literally.

OUT NOW!

TURN OVER TO READ
CHAPTER ONE!

Paperback: ISBN 978-1-903858-04-2
ePub: ISBN 978-1-903858-05-9

unSeen

FIND OUT MORE AT: WWW.IAMMARGARET.CO.UK

I AM MARGARE+

"Great style ... like The Hunger Games."
EOIN COLFER, author of *Artemis Fowl*

CORINNA TURNER

I AM MARGARET

CHAPTER 1

The dragon roared, its jaws so close to Thane's head that

I waggled the page gently in the air, waiting for my writing to dry. One final, blank double spread remained. Good. I'd made the little book myself.

The ink was dry. I turned to that last page and found the place on the computer printout I was copying from...

he felt his eardrums burst. But the sword had done its work and, eviscerated, the beast began to topple.

Thane rolled frantically to his feet and ran. The huge body obliterated where he'd been lying, but Thane wasn't interested in that. He kept right on running to where Marigold was struggling to free herself.

"That's the last time I go riding without my spurs!" she told him. "I could've cut my way out of here by now..."

Thane ignored her grumbles. He couldn't hear properly anyway. He whipped out a dagger and freed her. "Marigold?" He could hardly hear himself. "Are you all right?"

"Oh, I'm fine. At least I had my rosary."

Thane thought of all the things he wanted to say to her. The way he felt about her, he wanted to do everything just right. Could he get down on one knee without losing his balance and would he be able to hear what she said in reply...?

Then Marigold's arms wrapped around him like vines around their supporting tree. And when she kissed him, he knew the answer to all his questions was a heartfelt,

'Yes.'

I wrote the last word with great care and put the lid on the pen. All done. I smiled as I pictured Bane reading the tale. *Where are the slain dragons? Where are the rescued maidens?* he would complain after reading my stories. Just this once, in this tale just for him, there were all the dragons he could desire. But only one maiden.

A funny way to declare your love, but I couldn't leave it unsaid. And if I *did* pass my Sorting... well, we were both eighteen, we'd be leaving school at the end of the year and would be free to register, so perhaps it was time we were finally honest with each other.

Picking up the printout of the story, I ripped it into small pieces and threw it in the bin, then closed the handwritten book, slipping it into the waterproof pouch I'd made for it. On my aged—but no less loved for that—laptop, I called up the file and pressed 'delete'. Bane's story was his alone.

The pouch went into my bag as I checked its contents again. Clothes, underwear, sewing things, my precious bookReader—filled to capacity—and what little else was permitted. No laptop, alas, and no rosary beads for Margaret in this all too real world. I touched the waterproof pouch— must warn Bane not to show the story around. A dangerous word had slipped in there, near the end. A little bit of myself.

The contents of the bag were all present and correct, as they'd been since last night. Zipping it up, I stood for a moment, looking around. This had been my room since I was born and how I wanted to believe I'd be back here this evening, unpacking my bag again... But I'd never been very good at fairy tales. Happy Ever After didn't happen in real life. Not while you were alive.

I kicked at my long purple skirt for a moment, then picked up my jacket and slipped it on. Sorting day was a home clothes day. No need for school uniform at the Facility. I was packed and ready—packed, anyway—and couldn't delay any longer. I put my bag over my shoulder and headed downstairs.

My parents were waiting in the hall. I almost wished they weren't. That they were off with Kyle—*gone*.

Mum's face was so pale. "Margo, you can't seriously intend to go today..." Her voice was hoarse with desperation. "You know the chances of... of..."

"I know the chances of me passing are very small." With great effort I kept my voice from shaking. "But you know why I have to go."

"It's not too late..." Bleak hopelessness in Dad's voice. "The Underground would hide you..."

I had to get out of there. I had to get out before they wore down my resolve.

"It's too late to teach me to be selfish now," I snapped, switching automatically from Latin to English as I opened the front door and stepped out onto the step.

"Margo..."

I turned to meet Mum's embrace and I wanted to cling to her like a little girl, except that was how she was clinging to me. I stroked her hair and tried to comfort her. "It'll be all right, Mum, really," I whispered. "I might even pass, you know."

She released me at last, stepped back, mopping her eyes—trying to be strong for me. "Of course. You may pass. Keep the faith, darling." Her voice shook; right here, right now, she could hardly get the familiar words out.

"Keep the faith," said Dad, and his voice shook too.

I cupped my hand and made the Fish with finger and thumb, behind my bag so the neighbors couldn't see. "Keep the faith." It came out like an order. I blushed, smiled apologetically, took one last look at their faces and hurried down the steps.

The EuroBloc Genetics Department inspectors were

waiting at the school gates to check off our names. I joined the line, looking into the boys' schoolyard for Bane. A hotel car pulled up and a white-faced woman helped a tall boy from the back seat—who was *he?* His hair was like autumn leaves... oh. He held a long thin white cane with a soft ball on one end. Blind. My insides clenched in sympathy. What must it be like to have no hope at all?

"Name?" demanded the inspector on the boys' gate.

"Jonathan Revan," said the boy in a very cold, collected voice. "And wouldn't it be an awful lot simpler if my parents just dropped me at the Facility?"

The inspector looked furious as everyone sniggered their appreciation at this show of courage.

"Name?" It was my turn. The blind boy was passing through the gates, his shoulders hunched now, as though to block the sound of the woman's weeping. A man was shepherding her back to the car.

"Margaret Verrall."

The woman marked off my name and jerked the pen towards the girls' yard. "In."

Inside, I headed straight for the wall between the schoolyards. Bane was there, his matte black hair waving slightly in the breeze. His mother used to keep it short, to hide its strangeness, but that'd only lasted 'til he was fast enough to outrun her. The inspector on the boys' gate was shooting a suspicious glance at him.

"Looking forward to being an adult?" Bane asked savagely, watching Jonathan Revan picking his way across the schoolyard, his stick waving sinuously in front of him. Something clicked.

"That's your friend from out at Little Hazleton, isn't it? The preKnown, who's never had to come to school?"

"Yeah." Bane's face was grim.

"Did you hear what he said to the inspector? He's got some nerve."

"He's got that, all right. Shame he can't see a thing."

"He'd have to see considerably *more* than a thing to pass."

"Yeah." Bane kicked the wall, scuffing his boots. "Yeah, well, I always knew there was nothing doing."

"It was nice of you to be friends with him."

Bane looked embarrassed and kicked the wall even harder. "Well, he's got a brain the size of the EuroBloc main server. He'd have been bored out of his mind with only the other preKnowns to talk to."

Oh no, perhaps I flattered myself, but... if Bane was preoccupied with Jonathan Revan... he hadn't realized I was in danger! I should've said something—months, *years* ago. But no one talked about their Sorting. How could he not have *realized?* We'd known each other since, well, forever. He'd always been there, along with Mum and Dad, Kyle, Uncle Peter...

"Bane, I need to talk to you."

He looked around, his brown eyes surprised. He sat on the wall and rested his elbows on the railings. "Now? Not... after our Sorting?"

Were his thoughts running along the same lines as mine earlier? I sat down as well, which brought our faces very close. "Bane... it may not be very easy to talk... after."

His eyes narrowed. "What d'you mean?"

"Bane..." There was no easy way to say this. "Bane, I probably won't pass."

His face froze into incredulous disbelief—he really hadn't realized. He'd thought me Safe. *Bane, I'm so sorry...*

"You... of course you'll pass! You're as smart as Jon, you can keep the whole class spellbound, hanging on your every word..."

"But I can't do math to save my life."

There was a long, sick silence.

"Probably literally," I added, quite unnecessarily.

Bane remained silent. He saw the danger now. You only had to fail one single test. He looked at me at last and there was something strange in his eyes, something it took me a moment to recognize. Fear.

"Is it really *that* bad, your math?"

"It's almost non-existent," I said as gently as I could. "I have severe numerical dyslexia, you know that."

"I didn't realize. I just never..." There was guilt in his eyes, now; guilt that he'd gone through life so happy and confident in his physical and mental perfection that he'd

never noticed the shadow hanging over me. "Didn't Fa...
your Uncle Peter... teach you enough?"

"Uncle Peter managed to teach me more than anyone
else ever has, but I'm actually not sure it's possible to teach
me *enough*."

"I just never thought..."

"Of course you didn't think about it. Who thinks about
Sorting unnecessarily? Anyway, this is for you." I put the
pouch into his hand. "Don't let anyone see it until you've
read it; I don't think you'll want to flash it around."

His knuckles whitened around it. "Margo, what are you
doing here? If you think you're going to fail! Go, go now, I'll
climb over and distract the inspector; the Underground will
hide you..."

"Bane, stop, stop! I can't miss my Sorting, don't you
understand? There was never any way I was going to get
out of it—no one's allowed to leave the department with
preSort-age children and after today I'll show up as a
SortEvader on every system in the EuroBloc..."

"So go underground!" He dropped his voice to a whisper.
"You of all people could do that in an instant!"

"Yes, Bane, I could. And never mind spending the rest of
my life running, can't you see why I, *of all people*, cannot
run?"

He slammed his fist into the wall and blood sprung up
on his knuckles. "This is because of the Underground stuff,
isn't it? Your family are in too deep."

"Bane..." I captured his hand before he could injure it any
more. "You know the only way the sanctuary will stay
hidden is if the house *isn't* searched and if I run, what's the
first thing they'll do?"

"Search your house."

"Search my house. Arrest my parents. Lay a trap for the
next Underground members who come calling. Catch the
priests when they come. You know what they do to the
priests?"

"I know." His voice was so quiet I could hardly hear him.

"And you want that to happen to *Uncle* Peter? *Cousin*
Mark? How can you suggest I *run*?"

He said nothing. Finally he muttered, "I wish you'd given

this stuff up years ago..."

Bane had never understood my faith; he knew it would probably get me killed one day. He'd tried his hardest to talk me out of it before my sixteenth birthday, oh, how he'd tried. But he accepted it. He might not understand the faith angle, but getting killed doing something to piss off the EuroGov was right up his street.

The school bell began to ring and he looked up again, capturing my eyes. "I suppose then you wouldn't have been you," he murmured. "Look, if you don't pass..." his voice grew firmer, "if you don't pass, I'll have to see what I can do about it. Because... well... I've been counting on marrying you for a very long time, now, and I've no intention of letting anything stop me!"

My heart pounded—joy, but no surprise. How we felt about each other had been an unspoken secret for years. "Anything, such as the entire EuroBloc Genetics Department? Don't bite off more than you can chew, Bane."

He didn't answer. He just slipped an arm through the railings and snagged me, his lips coming down on mine. My arms slid through the railings, around his strong back, my lips melted against his and suddenly the world was a beautiful, beautiful place and this was the best day of my life.

We didn't break apart until the bell stopped ringing.

"Well," I whispered, looking into his brown eyes, "now I can be dismantled happily, anyway."

His face twisted in anguish. "Don't say that!" He kissed me again, fiercely. "Don't worry..." His hands cupped my face and his eyes glinted. "Whatever happens, *don't worry.* I love you and I *will not* leave you there, you understand?"

Planting one last kiss on my forehead, he swung his bag onto his shoulder and sprinted across the schoolyard, the pouch still clasped in his hand. I watched him go, then picked up my own bag and followed the last stragglers through the girls' door.

The classroom was unusually quiet, bags and small cases cluttering the aisles. Taking my place quickly, I glanced around. There were only two preKnowns in the class. Harriet looked sick and resigned, but Sarah didn't understand about her Sorting or the Facility or anything as complex as that. The known Borderlines were every shade of pale. The Safe looked sober but a little excited. The pre-Sorting ban on copulation would be gone tomorrow. No doubt the usual orgy would ensue.

Bane's last words stuck in my mind. I knew that glint in his eye. I should've urged him much more strenuously not to do anything rash. Not to put himself in danger. Now it was too late.

"I saw you and Bane," giggled Sue, beside me. "Jumping the gun a little, aren't you?"

"As if you haven't done any gun jumping yourself," I murmured. Sue just giggled even harder.

"Margy...? Margy...?"

"Hi, Sarah. Have you got your bag?"

Sarah nodded and patted the shabby bag beside her.

"They explained to you, right? That you'll be going on a sleep-over?"

Sarah nodded, beaming, and pointed at me. "Margy come too?"

"Perhaps. Only the most special children will be going, you know."

Sarah laughed happily. I swallowed bile and tried not to curse the stupid driver who'd knocked her down all those years ago and left her like this. Tried not to curse her parents, who'd put her into care, sued the driver for his Child Permittance so they could replace her, and promptly moved away.

"Children..." The deputy headmistress. She waited for quiet. "This is the last time I will address you as such. This is a very special day for you all. After your Sorting, you will be legally adults."

Except those of us who would scarcely any longer count as human. She didn't mention that bit.

"Now, do your best, all of you. Doctor Vidran is here from the EGD to oversee your Sorting. Over to you, Doctor Vidran..."

Doctor Vidran gave a long and horrible speech about the numerous benefits Sorting brought to the human race. By the time he'd finished I was battling a powerful urge to go up and shove his laser pointer down his throat. I managed to stay in my seat and concentrated on trying to love this misguided specimen of humanity, to forgive him his part in what was probably going to happen to me. It was very difficult.

"...A few of you will of course have to be reAssigned, and it is important that we always remember the immense contribution the reAssigned make, in their own way..."

Finally he shut up and bade us turn our attention to our flickery desk screens for the Intellectual Tests. My happiness at his silence took me through Esperanto, English, Geography, History, ComputerScience, Biology, Chemistry and Physics without hitch, but then came Math.

I tried. I really, really tried. I tried until I thought my brain would explode and then I thought about Bane and my parents and I tried some more. But it was no good. No motivation on earth could enable me to do most of those sums without a calculator. I'd failed.

The knowledge was a cold, hard certainty in the pit of my stomach all the way through the Physical Tests after a silent, supervised lunch. I passed all those, of course. Sight, Hearing, Physiognomy and so on, all well within the acceptable levels. What about Jonathan Revan, a preKnown if ever there was one? Smart, Bane said, really smart, and Bane was pretty bright himself. Much good it'd do Jonathan. Much good it'd do me.

We filed into the gym when it was all over, sitting on benches along the wall. Bane guided Jonathan Revan to a free spot over on the boys' side. In the hall through the double doors the rest of the school fidgeted and chatted. Once the end of semester assembly was over, they were free for four whole weeks.

Free. Would I ever be free again?

I'd soon know. One of the inspectors was wedging the doors open as the headmaster took his place on the stage. His voice echoed into the gym. "And now we must congratulate our New Adults! Put your hands together, everyone!"

Dutiful clapping from the hall. Doctor Vidran stood by

the door, clipboard in hand, and began to read names. A boy. A girl. A boy. A girl. Sorry, a young man, a young woman... Each New Adult got up and went through to take their seat in the hall. Was there a pattern...? No, randomized. Impossible to know if they'd passed your name or not.

My stomach churned wildly now. Swallowing hard, I stared across the gym at Bane. Jonathan sat beside him, looking cool as a cucumber, if a little determinedly so. *He* wasn't in any suspense. Bane stared back at me, his face grim and his eyes fierce. I drank in the harsh lines of his face, trying to carve every beloved detail into my mind.

"They might call my name," Caroline was whispering to Harriet. "They might. It's still possible. Still possible..."

Over half the class had gone through.

Still possible, still possible, they might, they might call my name... my mind took up Caroline's litany, and my desperate longing came close to an *ache...*

"Blake Marsden."

A knot of anxiety inside me loosened abruptly— immediately replaced by a more selfish pain. Bane glared at Doctor Vidran and didn't move from his seat. Red-faced, the deputy headmistress murmured in Doctor Vidran's ear.

Doctor Vidran looked exasperated. "Blake Marsden, known as Bane Marsden."

Clearly the best Bane was going to get. He gripped Jonathan's shoulder and muttered something, probably *bye.* Jonathan found Bane's hand and squeezed and said something back. Something like *thanks for everything.*

Bane shrugged this off and got up as the impatient inspectors approached him. *No... don't go, please...* Yes! He was heading straight for me—but the inspectors cut him off.

"Come on... Bane, is it? *Congratulations,* through you go..." Bane resisted being herded and the inspector's voice took on a definite warning note. "Now, you're an adult, it's your big day, don't spoil it..."

"I just want to speak to..."

They caught his arms. He wrenched, trying to pull free, but they were strong men and there were two of them.

"You *know* no contact is allowed at this point. I'm sure your girlfriend will be through in a moment."

"Fiancée," snarled Bane, and warmth exploded in my stomach, chasing a little of the chill fear from my body. He'd read my story already.

"*If*, of course, your *fiancée*," Doctor Vidran sneered the un-PC word from over by the door, "is a perfect specimen. If not, you're better off without her, *aren't* you?"

Bane's nostrils flared, his jaw went rigid and his knuckles clenched until I thought his bones would pop from his skin. Shoulders shaking, he allowed the inspectors to bundle him across the gym towards Doctor Vidran. *Uh oh...*

But by the time they reached the doors he'd got sufficient hold of himself he just stopped and looked back at me instead of driving his fist into Doctor Vidran's smug face. He seemed a long way away. But he'd never been going to reach me, had he?

'Love you...' he mouthed.

'Love you...' I mouthed back, my throat too tight for actual words.

Then a third inspector joined the other two and they shoved him through into the hall. And he was gone.

Gone. I might never see him again. I swallowed hard and clenched my fists, fighting a foolish frantic urge to rush across the gym after him...

"*Really*," one inspector was tutting, "we don't usually have to drag them *that* way!"

"Going to end up on a gurney, that one," apologized the deputy headmistress, "So sorry about that..."

Doctor Vidran dismissed Bane with a wave of his pen and went on with the list.

"They might..." whispered Caroline, "they might..."

They might... they might... I might be joining Bane. I might... Please...

But they didn't. Doctor Vidran stopped reading, straightened the pages on his clipboard and glanced at the other inspectors. "Take them away," he ordered.

He and the deputy headmistress swung round and went into the hall as though those of us left had ceased to exist. As we kind of had. The only decent thing to do about reAssignees was to forget them. Everyone knew that.

One of the inspectors took the wedges from under the

doors and closed them. Turned the key, locking us apart.

My head rang. I'd thought I'd known, I'd thought I'd been quite certain, but still the knowledge hit me like a bucket of ice-cold water, echoing in my head. Margaret Verrall. My name. They'd not called it. The last tiny flame of hope died inside me and it was more painful than I'd expected.

One of the boys on the bench opposite—Andrew Plateley—started crying in big, shuddering gasps, like he couldn't quite believe it. Harriet was hugging Caroline and Sarah was tugging her sleeve and asking what was wrong. My limbs felt heavy and numb, like they weren't part of me.

Doctor Vidran's voice came to us from the hall, just audible. "Congratulations, adults! What a day for you all! You are now free to apply for breeding registration, providing your gene scans are found to be compatible. I imagine your head teacher would prefer you to wait until after your exams next semester, though!"

The school laughed half-heartedly, busy sneaking involuntary glances to see who was left in the gym—until an Inspector yanked the blinds down over the door windows. Everyone would be glad to have us out of sight so they could start celebrating.

"After successful registration," the Doctor's cheerful voice went on, "you may have your contraceptive implants temporarily removed. The current child permittance is one child per person, so each couple may have two. Additional child permittances can be bought; the price set by the EGD is currently three hundred thousand Eurons, so I don't imagine any of you need to worry about that."

More nervous laughter from the hall. Normal life was through there. Exams, jobs, registering, having children, growing old with Bane... but I wasn't in there with him. I was out here. My stomach fluttered sickly.

"ReAssignees, up you get, pick up your bags," ordered one of the inspectors.

I got to my feet slowly and picked up my bag. My hands were shaking. Why did I feel so shocked? Had some deluded part of me believed this couldn't really happen? Around me everyone was moving as though in a daze, except Andrew Plateley who just sat, rocking to and fro, sobbing. Jonathan said something quietly to him but he didn't seem to hear.

The inspector shook Andrew's shoulder, saying loudly, "Up." He pointed to the external doors at the other end of the gym but Andrew leapt to his feet and bolted for the hall. Yanked at the doors with all his strength, sobbing, but they just rattled slightly under his assault and remained solidly closed. The inspectors grabbed him and began to drag him away, kicking and screaming. There was a sudden, suffocating silence from beyond those doors, as everyone tried not to hear his terror.

Doctor Vidran's voice rushed on, falsely light-hearted, "And I'm *sure* I don't need to remind you that you can only register with a person of your own ethnicity. Genetic mixes are, *of course*, not tolerated and all such offspring will be destroyed. And as you know, all unRegistered children automatically count as reAssignees from birth, but I'm sure you're all going to register correctly so none of you need to worry about anything like that."

They'd got Andrew outside and the inspectors were urging the rest of us after him. It seemed a terribly long way, my bag seemed to weigh a very great deal and I still felt sick. I swallowed again, my hand curving briefly, unseen, into the Fish. Be strong.

"And that's all from me, though your headmaster has kindly invited me to stay for your end of semester presentations. Once again, congratulations! Let's hear it for Salperton's New Adults...!"

The school whooped and cheered heartily behind us. A wave of crazy, reality-defying desperation swept over me—this must be how Andrew had felt. As though, if I could just get into that hall, *I'd* have the rest of my life ahead of me too...

Reality waited outside in the form of a little EGD minibus. Imagine a police riot van that mated with a tank. Reinforced metal all over, with grilles over the windows. Reaching the hall would achieve precisely *nothing*. So *get a grip, Margo*.

I steadied Sarah as she scrambled into the minibus and passed my bag up to her. She busied herself lifting my bag and hers onto the overhead luggage racks, beaming with pride at her initiative.

"Thanks, Sarah." A soft white ball wandered into my vision—there was Jonathan Revan, the last left to get in after me. I almost offered help, then thought better of it. "Jonathan, isn't it? Just give a shout if you want a hand."

"Thanks, Margaret." His eyes stared rather eerily into the minibus. Or rather, through the minibus, for they focused not at all. "I'm fine."

His stick came to rest against the bus's bumper and his other hand reached out, tracing the shape of the seats on each side, then checking for obstructions at head height. Just as the EGD inspectors moved to shove him in, he stepped up into the bus with surprising grace. I climbed in after him just as the school fire alarms went off, the sound immediately muffled by the inspectors slamming the doors behind me.

"Bag?" Sarah was saying to Jonathan, holding out her hand.

"Sorry?"

"Bag," I told him. "Would you like her to put your bag up?"

"Oh. Yes, thank you. What's your name?"

"Sarah."

"Sarah. Thanks."

Bet he wouldn't have let me put his bag up for him! Sarah sat down beside Harriet, so I took a seat next to Jonathan. The first pupils were spilling out into the school-yards and I craned my neck to try and catch a glimpse of Bane. A last glimpse.

"Any guesses who set that off?" said Jonathan dryly.

"Don't know how he'd have done it, but yeah, I bet he did."

The minibus began to move, heading for the gates, and I twisted to look out the rear window, through the bars. Nothing...

We pulled onto the road and finally there he was, streaking across the schoolyard to skid to a halt in front of the gates just as they slid closed. Bane gripped them as though he wanted to shake them, rip them off their hinges or throw them open...

The minibus went around a corner and he was gone.

ABOUT THE AUTHOR

Corinna Turner has been writing since she was fourteen and likes strong protagonists with plenty of integrity. She has an MA in English from Oxford University, but has foolishly gone on to work with both children and animals! Juggling work with the disabled and being a midwife to sheep, she spends as much time as she can in a little hut at the bottom of the garden, writing.

She is a Catholic Christian with roots in the Methodist and Anglican churches. A keen cinema-goer, she lives in the UK. She used to have a Giant Snail called Peter with a 6½" long shell, but now makes do with a cactus and a campervan!

Get in touch with Corinna...

Facebook/Google+: Corinna Turner

Twitter: @CorinnaTAuthor

or sign up for **news** and **free short stories**, including 'An Unexpected Guest'—about Kyle (and Joe!)— at: *www.IAmMargaret.co.uk*

DOWNLOAD YOUR EBOOK

If you own a paperback of *Brothers* you can download a free copy of the eBook.

1. Go to *www.IAmMargaret.co.uk* or scan the QR code:

2. Enter this code: KAJ7773G

3. Enjoy your download!

All Free/Exclusive content subject to availability.